BOB THE ZOMBIE

BOOK THREE

JOHN P. LOGSDON

CHRISTOPHER P. YOUNG

CRIMSON MYTH
PRESS

Published by: Crimson Myth Press (www.CrimsonMyth.com)

Edited by: Lorelei J. Logsdon (www.LoreleiLogsdon.com)

Cover art: Jake T. Logsdon (www.JakeLogsdon.com) & Ric Lumb (www.PuttyCad.co.uk)

HIGHWAYWOMAN

*M*odacio stood at the edge of the road, looking toward town. It was common knowledge that Teggins, the current head of the Thieves Union in Dakmenhem, was the mold for punctuality. Fortunately, he was also one that went for outmoded forms of transportation, which meant he'd be easy to ambush.

Her first thought had been to go straight up to the Burnt Amber Tavern and just ask to see him, but there was something about having a contract on your head worth 50,000 in gold that made you question the logic of showing your face at the headquarters of the Thieves Union.

"Him der yet?" asked Modacio's counterpart, Kone, a massive gray Ogre with jutting teeth and rippling muscles who had stepped out onto the road and was looking directly into the sunlight that cascaded through his wisps of hair.

"Get back behind the trees, you idiot."

Kone sulked back. "Sorry."

Modacio shook her head in wonderment at why an Ogre of such incredible stupidity would want to get into a life of thieving. Then she paused and was forced to ask herself why she had hired such an Ogre.

Kone wasn't all that bad once you figured out how to work with him. The key thing he brought to the table was brawn. Modacio had the brains, and while she was also quite capable with an assortment of weaponry, not to mention hand-to-hand combat, she lacked that imposing hugeness that Kone carried naturally. Plus, Kone had been gifted with a specific skill that sometimes came in handy. He could knock a person in the head with a carefully controlled force that would erase their memory back a certain amount of time. She hadn't believed it when they'd first met, but after seeing him in action a few times, she offered him a partnership. It wasn't technically a *partnership*, but Ogres don't take well to having bosses, per se, being that they're quite into socialism. But Modacio made sure that Kone understood that their partnership was the kind where he did what she said, not because she was the boss, but because she had the brains. He was leery at first, but warmed up to the idea when she explained he would be receiving a "boss-level share" at 10-percent of all earnings.

"Damn," she said under her breath. "I'm sorry, Kone. You know I don't really think you're an idiot. I'm just a bit stressed out right now."

"Dat's okay," he replied with a childlike smile.

Another peek around the tree and Modacio saw that the carriage was coming along right on schedule.

"They're coming," she said. "You remember what you're supposed to do?"

"Yep. Stand here until you call me. Den I s'posed ta growl and stuff if dey gives you any trouble."

"And...?"

"Oh, yeah, if dey get da better of you, I'm s'posed ta knock dem in der heads and make dem forget stuff."

"Right," Modacio said as Kone unfurrowed his brow and groaned like someone who had just barely passed a placement exam.

∽

Grubby Longthumper irritably bounced around in the back of the carriage.

Why Teggins insisted on these traditionalisms was beyond Grubby. It had to be due to the fact that Teggins simply didn't trust the newer modes of transport. Grubby had heard something about how the man's mother and father met with their doom during an Ogre bike ride in Fez, but he'd never got the full skinny on the story.

All Grubby knew was that, as a Dark Halfling, the bumpiness of a carriage ride was not fun. Worse, it didn't help that he had to sit facing the back because Teggins took up the majority of the seat that faced forward.

Along with his fat wallet, Teggins also had a sizable gut. To be more clear, when the horses saw Teggins climbing in for his daily ride, they knew they were in for a workout. Regardless of his interesting shape, Grubby was certain that there was a fair amount of muscle tucked under the rolls of fat because Teggins was quite capable of pushing both Orcs and Ogres around, and not just verbally.

Grubby considered Teggins just as much of a jerk as he considered most Humans.

The man was in a constant state of surliness, which was one of only a few redeeming qualities. Since Dark Halflings grew up in a world where surliness was a way of life, Grubby understood his boss. It should be noted that this did not mean that Grubby trusted Teggins. Far from it. But it should also be noted that as a Dark Halfling, Grubby was carefully reared to make sure he trusted no one.

"Grubby," said Teggins in his gruff voice, "you got the paperwork on Treneth of Dahl handy?"

The Dark Halfling open his magical leather attache case and whispered "Treneth of Dahl" into it. An instant later the papers stuck out of the top, ready to be plucked. Grubby was not one to waste money on trinkets and fads, but he considered his briefcase as one of the best investments he'd ever made. He loved its leathery feel, and the merchant he'd gotten it from had gone to far lengths to make it match the tint of blue that composed Grubby's skin. It was a nice touch. His ePad was also an incredible asset, but Teggins refused to use that sort of technology, and that meant Grubby had to keep actual paperwork at-the-ready.

"Good," Teggins said, taking the sheets and looking them over. "He's still with Curlang Jetherby, I see."

"Looks like."

"Seems they've been inseparable since spending all that time together in prison."

"Inseparable is a good word to describe it," Grubby said with a menacing chuckle.

Teggins glanced over the top of the paper with a squint. "Ah," he said without changing his expression even slightly. "Humor?"

Grubby grunted. "Apparently not."

"Maybe we ought to invite Treneth down here for a bit." Teggins stroked his tightly-trimmed, graying beard while taking a thoughtful glance out the window. "We could always do with using a wizard's skills, especially since we're now on somewhat even ground with each other after the fight we had and all."

"He ain't gonna come down here without Jetherby."

"Yeah, that's a problem," noted Teggins. "Of course, I *could* clear his name if he underwent the proper reprimand process."

"Would do him good to get a whipping."

Teggins nodded. "Don't know I can trust him, though."

"Especially not if he has a wizard that's more invested in his interests than in the Union's."

"Exactly." Teggins handed back the papers and sighed. "Well, something to think about, anyway."

Just as Grubby was slipping the papers back into his pouch, he heard a shout and a cracking noise. The carriage was slowing down, making things more bumpy.

"Stop this infernal thing," he could hear a female voice demanding, "or I'll slit your throat as surely as you sit there!"

Teggins groaned and looked at his timepiece. "Looks like we're being robbed."

"Highwaymen," Grubby confirmed with distaste.

"Highway*woman* from the sound of it."

"Right, I just meant…never mind."

"Obviously new to the area," said Teggins. "Break out one of the Thieves Union membership forms so that we can get things settled."

Grubby did so and also grabbed a pen in the process.

The door swung open and Grubby saw a face that he'd seen before. He'd seen it many times, in fact. This is what happened when you were responsible for setting an ever-increasing price on the head of someone that the Union wanted dead. But it wasn't her head that helped solidify that Grubby was indeed a member of the Longthumper family, meaning that he reacted in a way that all the men in his clan do when they saw a woman such as her. It was her athletic build, tight clothes, and midnight black hair. Not that her

5

face was at all bad, mind you. She was quite the looker, even to the likes of a Dark Halfling.

"Modacio?" Teggins said and then cackled in his weighty kind of way. "You've got guts coming here."

"It couldn't be helped," she replied.

"Makes things easier, don't you think, Grubby?"

Grubby whipped a blade out of one of his Frebblyskin boots with the speed of a viper. An instant later the point of the blade was pressed against her jugular.

"Looks like my second-in-command here is interested in that bounty, Modacio."

"I'm...I'm here to offer you a deal," she said raggedly.

If Teggins had a weak spot, other than handfuls of sweets and dishes of gravy, it was the prospect of a deal. Many heads were saved over the years on account of making a deal with Teggins. Grubby was one of the few who understood this about his boss's nature. He doubted that Modacio knew about this personality quirk, but, assuming that the deal was worthwhile, luck was on her side.

"I'm listening," Teggins said with a tilt of his head and a wave of his hand.

Grubby lowered the knife and casually slid it back into his boot. Then he patted the seat beside him and Modacio cautiously sat down.

"Do you remember the Zomboner Corporation?" she said, after a moment.

"The one that made the willy pills?" asked Grubby.

Modacio looked down at him. "Willy pills?"

"Makes the ding-ding poke up when it don't wanna."

"Yes, those," Modacio said before turning back to Teggins. "Anyway, everyone knows that they ultimately failed, and I'm more than certain that thousands of men were sad about that, but I know *why* they failed."

"And you think that by telling me why they failed that I'm going to spare your head?" Teggins said with piercing eyes.

Modacio swallowed hard. "What I'm offering is this: I do everything that's necessary to get the Zombie parts, go through the processes, including the one that Zomboner Corp was missing—the one that caused them to fail—and bring you back a finished product that actually works."

Teggins gave her a tight stare. "Are you saying you think I need a little lift?"

Grubby fought to hold back a laugh.

"Huh? Ohhh…no, no no," Modacio replied in a rush, waving her hands dramatically. "A man of your, uh, stature? Surely not!"

"That's right," Teggins said, looking from side to side. "I'm doing *just* fine in that department, let me tell you."

"I'm sure you are," Modacio said. "No doubt at all."

There was a moment of uncomfortable silence.

"Anyway," she continued, "while you are, I would imagine, above and beyond the virility level of the average, well, man, there are thousands of men who would drop heavy sums of coin to get a bit of help for their…uh—"

"Willy," Grubby offered helpfully.

Modacio smiled nervously and nodded with a shrug.

"Hmmm," said Teggins as the air grew thick in the carriage.

Even though Grubby had seen Teggins in negotiations countless times, there was just something about the way the man applied critical thinking that gave those around him the feeling that something was about to come undone. The flood of facial contortions and barely audible grunts and incessant mumbling was most unnerving. And once he got started, there was no stopping him until he reached his final

7

conclusion, which, by all accounts, would be final. It was a rare thing that Teggins left anything to chance.

"Gnff…fneff…grumble…" said Teggins in his own world.

"There goes that, then," said Grubby in a gruff whisper.

"What's he…doing?"

"Thinking."

"Hnng…krem…baff̀…"

"Is that what that is?"

"Easier for some than others, I suppose," Grubby answered.

"Moop…vlek…denbo…cim…"

"It's a solid plan," she began toward Teggins, but Grubby pulled on her arm and shushed her. "I'm trying to give him additional—"

"Won't matter," Grubby interrupted. "He never starts into this kind of mental percolation unless he's got enough info. If you add anything to the mix, it'll just prove to take him longer. Plus, usually when people offer more information, he ends up giving a no. So unless you want today to be the day where you find it really challenging to wear a hat, you'd be best to just leave him to it for now."

"Why would I find it challenging to wear a hat?"

"Hard to put on a hat when you ain't got a head."

"Ah, I see."

"Ngrad…oolock…snako…woongie…"

"But if I could just explain the numbers that I've found, it'd make his mind up right away."

"Look, babe," said Grubby with a grimace, "he knows all about the finances. You don't get to our height in this biz without knowing the value of things. That ain't the issue. Problem is that he don't trust you, and rightly so. You did cause the last boss to end up in the clink."

"That was an accident," she said quietly.

"Idoo…wep…pew…oodi…"

"You led the cops right to the guy's place!" Grubby pointed out. "And let's not forget that you done that after you dropped the Diamond of Zoolah in his lap."

"I thought that's what I was supposed to do."

"Agoot? Agat?"

They paused their discussion as Teggins seemed to be asking questions.

"Ustoo…yem…blee!"

"Anyway," Grubby continued, "leading the cops to your boss's place is *never* what you're supposed to do."

"I didn't know they were following me."

"But they did follow you and that's why your head is worth so much."

"I know," she said, sullen. "Like I said, it was an accident."

For some reason, Grubby believed her. Probably because she had a great rack. Regardless, her head was worth a good 50k in gold. A Dark Halfling could see a lot of great racks with 50k in gold.

"Shwip…schwap…schwoop…"

"Ah," Grubby said with an accomplished look, "he's starting to finish up now."

"How can you tell?"

"Glip…glap…gloop…"

"Oh," Modacio said. "I hear it, yes."

"Frip…frap…froop…"

And just like that, Teggins was back in the world. His eyes refocused on Modacio and his eyebrows closed in on one another.

"Here's what we're gonna do," Teggins said in his dominant way. "You're gonna get this boner medication set up like you said and you're gonna get a lot of it. I can see millions in gold pouring in for a product like that. If it

9

works, your name gets cleared and you can rejoin the Thieves Union. No harm, no foul. But if you fail, or if it doesn't work, then the price on your head doubles."

"Plus my cut?" she said hopefully.

"Cut of what?"

"Sales?"

"Not gonna happen. The only cut you're getting is the one that happens if you don't bring back them pills."

"Right," she said nervously. "Can't blame a girl for trying."

"Sure I can," Teggins said.

"Can I at least have a pass until this mission is done?"

"I'll clear your contract for a while. You'll get safe passage from my crew, but only if you stick to the mission."

"How are we gonna know if she sticks to the mission?" said Grubby.

"I thought of that," said Teggins, keeping his eyes on Modacio. "I'm going to send one of my men with her to keep tabs on every move she makes. He'll report everything back to me. If she makes one slip-up, the bounty doubles."

"Who's it gonna be, then?" Grubby said, putting pen to paper.

"You."

"Yu Wazan?" Grubby replied with a nod. "He's in Pren on business. I'm sure I can get in touch with him through normal channels." He pointed at the paper. "Not this old crap you insist we keep using."

"No, not Yu," said Teggins. "You."

"Oh, you mean Redler Yu of the West Wanderers. Haven't seen him in years. A bit of dullard, if you ask me."

"Grubby," Teggins said, leaning forward enough to make the carriage whine slightly as he poked a chubby finger at the Dark Halfling's chest, "*you* are going with her."

Grubby bridled. "Me?"

Teggins sat back. "Yep. And I want everything documented." Then Teggins looked back at Modacio and said, "If you do anything stupid, he'll tell me. And if you do anything to him to make him not tell me, I'll know because he won't have told me nothin'."

"But what if there's nothing to tell?"

"Then he'll tell me that."

"Fine," she said while nodding. "I accept the terms."

"Wasn't like you had much of a choice," said Teggins. "Now, get out of my carriage. I'll speak with Grubby before he leaves."

Modacio stepped out without a further word.

Grubby knew what this was all about. Teggins was always looking for ways to get the Dark Halfling out of the office. Grubby knew too much about the Thieves Union and that made him a threat. It wasn't like it was his fault. How could he help but stumble upon information when he was thumbing around the offices in the middle of the night holding a tiny flashlight?

"Before you go getting all riled up, Grubby," Teggins said, "you're the man for the job. I don't trust very many people and I know that you trust even fewer."

Grubby sort of shrug-nodded, being that it *was* true.

"But if she really does have access to the final step and she can really pull it together, we'll be rich. I'm not talking wealthy, here. I'm talking rich. The kind of rich where wealthy people look at you in the hopes that you'll drop them some of your table scraps."

"Uh-huh," said Grubby, not believing that crap one bit. "Or it could be that you just don't like me being around the office all that much."

"I'm sure that has nothing to do with it," said Teggins with a cough. Then he clasped his hands and began rubbing them

JOHN P. LOGSDON & CHRISTOPHER P. YOUNG

together. "Regardless of my motivation, you're the man for the job. You might want to put an immediate halt on the removal of Modacio's head since I'm sure any heads floating next to hers will be duly chopped off as a matter of course."

"Yeah," Grubby said, purposefully opening his ePad, something that Teggins forbade in his carriage.

There was a pause that let Grubby know it had indeed bothered his current boss.

Finally, Teggins said, "once she brings back the pills and everything checks out, we'll knock her off and be done with it."

"She's not going to tell us anything," argued Grubby. "If she *does* get the pills, that'll be all we get out of her, I'd bet."

"We'll get the info," said Teggins with a ghastly grin.

"How can you be so sure?"

"Because I'll have my key man there taking notes the entire time."

Grubby rolled his eyes and started to step out of the carriage. "You can double-cross her all you want, Teggins," he said, "but if you try to stick a knife in my back, you know how that's going to end."

"You being dead on account of a knife in your back?"

"I think you know my capabilities better than that," Grubby said coldly.

"All right, little man," said Teggins with a hiss. "You just remember who your boss is."

"For now," Grubby said and then he jumped down onto the gravel road. "For now."

MAKING PROGRESS

$\mathcal{D}$epression was the leading cause of decay in Zombies, according to the research done by the renowned psychologist, Dr. Bunk Mozatto.

The rest of the scientific community had found flaws in his research, pointing out that there was plenty of documented evidence suggesting that the *real* leading cause of physical deterioration in Zombies was, well, being a Zombie.

Dr. Mozatto, an Orc by nature, disagreed, sort of. What *he* meant was that depression was the number one cause of accelerating their already accelerated rate of disrepair. To be fair, he noted, other races decayed over time, too, Zombies just did so in a near-eternal sort of way.

In an effort to prove his theory, Dr. Mozatto had done a double-blind study where he took two blind Zombies and checked their emotional states and their average daily decay rate over a three week period. He'd had them "watch" soundless GnomeTube videos for three hours a day over the course of yet another three weeks while also keeping tabs on their flesh-drop rate. Then he compared those values.

His findings suggested that having blind Zombies watch mute videos proved inconclusive.

On a whim, he tried another test where he did the same measurements, but instead of using videos as a means of testing, he had one of the subjects smile for 20 minutes twice a day. His thinking was based on noticing that when some of his normal patients seemed happy on certain days, they were smiling more. After reading a few books on mood and smiling, topics that were not discussed all that much at the Orc Institute of Psychology, he thought that maybe there was some correlation. Sure enough, the Zombie that smiled more often had a significantly lower rot-rate than the one who didn't smile at all. Lack of teeth notwithstanding, the act of twisting one's face into a smiling pose seemed effective.

The Ononokin Psychological Society awarded him with a medal for his research, making him the go-to guy for Zombies who were seeking treatment. Unfortunately, this wasn't exactly a boon to his business since the Zombie population was less than 500 in all of Ononokin, last checked, and most of them didn't bother with learning about awards handed out by the Ononokin Psychological Society, especially not to an Orc psychologist who was practicing in the Dark Halfling land of Dogda.

Bob had read Dr. Mozatto's biography at least fifty times since he began visiting. There was not much else to do when sitting in a waiting room, after all, especially for a Zombie. He was discouraged from picking up magazines since other patients, and the general populace, believed the misconception that Zombieism was contagious.

It wasn't.

The only way to contract Zombieism was the same way that Bob got it, which was to be bitten by a Vampire.

The Coalition Against The Proliferation Of Zombies

(CATPOZ) had sworn that the only way you could catch Zombieism was to bitten by a Zombie.

This misinformation, and the CATPOZ organization itself, was due to a public relations firm hired by both Viq and Vaq—the two predominant homes of Vampires—that had been hired to work on the image of Vampires. It was the only thing that the two countries ever worked on together, as they thoroughly despised each other.

But the CATPOZ statement was patently false. All one had to do to diffuse the logic was to look into the mouth of a Zombie. They had no teeth!

CATPOZ argued that the undead rotters may be lacking in the way of teeth, but, being that deviousness was in their nature—provable by the fact that they'd obviously tricked death, at least metaphysically speaking, and purposefully exempting the fact that Vampires did the same thing— Zombies assuredly could have worked out how to have pointy gums.

Bob recalled the day he was infected. It was some 17 years ago when he was nearing his 30th birthday. A stunningly attractive Vampire had come into town explaining the virtues and long-life benefits of Vampireness —an elite club of superior beings that could pursue most any dream because of their extreme length of life. All Bob had to do was sign the forms and take part in the ritual. It was a good time to be alive because the Vampires were only allowed to do induction rituals once every 100 years. Bob had signed the papers without reading them, paid the obligatory coins, and then felt the sharp, stabbing pain of fangs before he passed out.

Two days later he awoke to sad-looking faces.

"So rare," they were saying. "Such a shame."

Instead of becoming a Vampire, as the salesperson had

promised, Bob's immune system had fought the Vampirism and converted the incoming virus into Zombieism.

"One in a million chance," the Vampire's said.

He'd tried to sue, but the fine print on the papers he signed had explained that this was one of the many risks of undergoing the procedure.

"Bob!" the nurse chirped, bringing Bob back to the present.

"Oh," Bob said as he carefully got out of his chair so as not to leave any loose parts of his person behind. "Sorry."

She smiled in that not-so-friendly way that Bob had grown used to. "The doctor will see you now."

Dr. Mozatto peered over his wire-rimmed glasses as Bob walked in. It looked rather strange to see glasses on such a ghastly looking Orc.

Orcs were, generally speaking, not the most kind creatures. Dr. Mozatto had always betrayed this stereotype, once you got past the fact that he was exceedingly tall and muscular, had jutting teeth, a perpetually angry stare, an incessant habit of cracking his knuckles, a bit of that Orcish lack of verbal filter where they said what they were thinking regardless of the circumstances, and the fact that he grunted a lot.

"Have you been doing your smiling exercises, Bob?" Dr. Mozatto asked in his doctorly way as he motioned Bob to lie down on the plastic-covered couch.

Bob sighed and then gingerly lowered himself. He was envious of those who got to relax on the much larger couch that sat on the other side of the room. It was nice and leathery whereas his assigned lounger was tucked in the corner and was full of lumps.

"Most of the time," Bob replied, his mouth making a watery sound with each word. "I find it difficult to remember when so much of the world is, frankly, just horrible."

Dr. Mozatto grunted and started writing. "Stupid Zombie don't follow directions," he said, speaking as he wrote, which Bob often found only furthered his depression, "At this rate he'll be completely rotted away in half the time of a normal Zombie." He looked back up and said, "You gotta do the things I tells ya, Bob. If you don't stick with the plan, you ain't gonna get any better."

"I know," Bob said as if he believed the good doctor, which he didn't. "It's just, well, imagine spending your days avoiding everyone because they all say how bad you smell."

"I'm an Orc, Bob."

"Oh, right. Well, okay, but do you wake up with pieces of your flesh missing?"

"Rarely."

"It's rare when I don't," Bob said tiredly. "And that assumes that I can even get to sleep."

"Sleepy pills not working?"

"No," Bob stated with a shake of his head. It had said right on the bottle that the pills would not work for Zombies due to their inability to absorb the chemicals needed to induce sleep.

"Maybe try warm milk?"

Bob wanted to argue, but saw no point. The man who was supposed to be the authority on Zombies had little clue in regard to their physiology, even if he was mildly helpful from a psychological standpoint. Mostly, Bob had decided to start these appointments because he believed it was a way for him to express his frustration to someone who would not judge him. Too bad for Bob that he had selected an Orc for a doctor.

"Anyway," Bob said, ignoring the suggestion, "the lack of

sleep, the fact that people avoid me wherever I go, and the reality that I can barely hold down even the simplest job, just makes me wonder why I even bother to go on."

"Patient is showing signs of being suic…soo…s…o…u…" Dr. Mozatto paused his writing and looked around the room as if thinking, and then his brow furrowed and he refocused on his little book. He scratched at the pad back and forth and then continued his notes. "Patient wants to do himself in. Won't, though, 'cause he's a chicken. Well, he's a Zombie, really, but I'm just using the word 'chicken' to point out that he ain't really gonna do himself in."

Bob sighed again. Truth was that Dr. Mozatto was right. Bob wouldn't actually do anything that would end his own life. Not on purpose, anyway. As bad as life was sometimes, it was nothing compared to the lengths a Zombie would have to go to end it all.

"You still having them pigeon dreams, Bob?"

"Sometimes."

"They changed at all or are they the same?"

"Recently the pigeons have stopped pecking at my eyes."

"Well, that's something, at least."

"Now they peck at my brain instead."

"Hmmm," the doctor said in a grunting way. "I will have to check with my dream specialist to see what that means." He jotted something down and then looked back up. "How's the paranoia going?"

"It's still there," Bob answered. "Hard for it not to be when everyone looks at me the way they do, like they want me dead."

"Technically, Bob—"

"I know, I know, but you know what I mean." Against his better judgment, he plodded on. "And there's that special that was on a few months ago about people using Zombie parts for medicinal purposes."

"We talked about this before, Bob," Dr. Mozatto said like a father speaking to a child that was finding it hard to sleep due the absolute belief that there was a monster living under its bed.

"Yeah," Bob replied gloomily, "but it's just…sick, you know? I mean, it's like we're second-class citizens."

"I hate to be the bearer of bad news, Bob," said the doctor, "but you're kinda more like a dead citizen."

"Undead," Bob corrected him.

"Semantics," Dr. Mozatto said with a shrug. "Point is that you ain't quite even at the second-class level, if you catch my drift."

Bob did. It had been a struggle since day one of his infection. He'd tried to get a lawyer to represent him against the Vampires. His argument was that the print regarding the possibility of Zombieism was in a font so small that you'd need one of those fancy Gnome-built microscopes to even read it. Not a single lawyer would take the case, though, stating that there were no actual rights that they could defend for someone who had already passed on.

"Besides, Bob, some of them medicines have made lives better. The living type of lives, I mean."

"Right," Bob said, sinking down in his depressed way. "Who cares about the poor Zombie losing a finger as long as some snot-nosed Dwarf ends up with a clear complexion?"

"See? Now you're getting the contribution that you can bring to the table as a people."

"Sure, sure, sure," Bob said with his hands in the air, "and let's not forget about the improvement that one Zombie donated, via his entire leg, when the Ogres under the Greyogre transit system ran into that epidemic of a toenail fungus that caused them a bit of mild discomfort. And, it should be noted that when I say 'donate' what I really mean is that it was ripped from his person without so much as a how-do-ya-do?"

Dr. Mozatto was beaming. "I gotta say, Bob, you're startin' to show signs of improvement today!"

"Hard not to, doc! I mean, just think of how the Zomboner Corporation took all sorts of chunks out of Zombies in order to create their wonderful erectile dysfunction treatment pills."

"Elfagra," Dr. Mozatto said slowly, with a faraway look. "It's a shame they never got that product to work. The science for it was there. They just couldn't, excusing the pun, pull it off. Poor guys that were part of the test-case, though." The doctor shook his head mournfully. "Could you imagine waking up one day and finding your ding-ding was missing?"

Bob looked at him blankly. "Couldn't imagine it, doc."

"Horrible."

Ding!

"Ah, well, time's up," Dr. Mozatto said. "Have a good week, Bob. Remember, you gotta do those smile exercises if you wanna slow down the, uh, shedding process."

As Bob walked out he could hear the doctor finishing up his notes. "Patient made decent progress today. Not on the hygiene front, of course. Still smells like a rotting corpse, which I suppose makes sense. And people tell me *I* smell bad!"

Bob shut the door and found his way out of the building and into the overcast world that matched perfectly with the way he felt about his mere existence.

It seemed that even the droplets of rain made right-angles to avoid touching his skin.

A DAY AT THE PARK

*P*erkder Stonepebble wasn't the type of Dwarf
that liked being underground. He found it dark
and dismal, not to mention stuffy and somewhat smelling of
Dwarf. His world was full of bright colors, long walks,
beaches, dancing, sunshine, and a true love of wearing all
sorts of costumes as befitted whatever the monthly activity
was for the *CosPlay Posse*, a group of costume wearers of
which he was a founding member.

His shift at the famous Halfly's Park was closing in and
that was a sad thing for the likes of Perkder. Unlike the
majority of employees at the park, Perkder enjoyed the
customers. He had fun helping them find rides and cakes and
cones and whatever else they wanted to keep their chocolaty
adventure going. Plus, he got to wear all sorts of costumes
while on the job.

"Perkder," Finver Snickings, his supervisor, called out as
Perkder was putting away his things.

"Yes?" Perkder called back operatically.

Finver sneered as he always did. "Get in my office."

"On my way!" Perkder said and then commenced to

JOHN P. LOGSDON & CHRISTOPHER P. YOUNG

skipping toward the main building.

He patted a child on the head as he bounced and twisted merrily through the crowds of people. They were all giggling or even outright laughing at the sight of a Dwarf acting so bubbly. Perkder felt his spirits soar at this because he loved nothing more than to make people smile. Well, except maybe wearing costumes.

Perkder took the steps two at a time and glided in to Finver's office, saying "Ta-Da!"

Finver grunted, pointed at the chair in front of his desk, and said, "Sit."

Perkder sat and looked across at the gruff little man. While Perkder was a bit on the large side for a Dwarf, Finver was rather small for a Dark Halfling. He was completely bald, which was odd, and he was the only one of his kind that Perkder could recall seeing who was in constant need of a shave. It begged the question of whether or not Finver was fully Dark Halfling.

"We need to talk about your behavior again," Finver said tiredly.

"Oh?"

"You're not upholding the tradition that built Halfly's Park from nothing to what it is today. Everyone else does their job here like they're supposed to. But you...well, you either have to get it fixed or get another job."

Perkder winced. What had he done wrong? He thought over the day to see if anything stuck out as odd. He'd saved one little girl from the log flume, where she'd fallen directly into the deep end of the spill off; he'd helped a young couple find true love by suggesting that they check out The Dastardly Dungeon, a ride that had a tendency of causing lots of hand holding; he'd led a small, makeshift parade from one end of the park to the other, bringing smiles to easily fifty people who had joined the procession; he'd helped a portly fellow find a few packets of relish....ah-hah!

"Is it the relish thing?" he asked. "I mean, that poor man was completely unaware that Halfly's is opposed to the use of relish. He was on the brink of returning his smeared meat sandwich and storming off, but I remembered that I'd had a couple of packets leftover from when I had gone to Spinty's Buffet the other night for one of my monthly dress ups." He sighed and bobbed around for a moment. "I know it was the wrong thing to do, but I was just trying to make the customer happy."

Finver pointed at him. "And therein lies the problem."

"The relish, then. Well, I can only offer—"

"No, not the relish. Who cares about the relish?"

Pekder pointed at the sign that hung next to the window. It read, "No Damn Relish!" Everyone knew that Dark Halflings had an innate disgust for relish. Some people attributed it to the sensitiveness of their taste buds. It was those buds, after all, that allowed the little folks to make the most amazing sweets in the land.

"Yeah, well, right," Finver said, "but that ain't what I'm talking about right now. I'm talking about all your infernal helpfulness. All that dancing and prancing and singing, if you can really call it singing—you should seriously consider voice lessons, by the way—-and all the other...well...*happy* things you do."

Perkder smashed his lips together and closed one eye. "So you're saying that I'm *too* pleasant?"

"Of course you are! Haven't you ever met any of your own kind? You're not supposed to be happy. No Dwarfs are supposed to be happy!"

"Actually, there was one rather famous one that went by that—"

"A *proper* Dwarf," interrupted Perkder, "is one who is loud, boisterous, and in a constant state of having a chip on his shoulder. He grunts a lot. He glares a lot. He doesn't smile unless he's asking someone to see if there's something in his teeth. You're not like that. You're...you're a disgrace to Dwarfdom!"

Perkder leaned back in his chair, trying to keep his mood pleasant.

"Let me get this straight," Perkder said with one eye squinted, "you're saying that you don't want me to be so helpful?"

"Right."

"You don't like it when I make customers happy."

"It's a horrible way to run a business."

"You're telling me that the people who bring money into the park are to be treated poorly, groaned at, and made to feel like they're in a constant state of wasting my time?"

"Now you're getting it."

Perkder was amazed. "And you find that acting like that is better for repeat business than to show people a fun time?"

"I think that's obvious," said Finver with a tilt of his head. "Halfly's Park has been in business for more years than any other company in all of Ononokin. We have record years *every* year."

"Easy to do with the bar being set so low."

"What's that?"

"Nothing," Perkder said with an innocent smile. "You were saying?"

"The point is that we didn't get to where we are by going out of our way to make some snotty little brat smile!"

"I'm sorry," Perkder said, feeling awfully confused, "but I'm really not getting it."

Finver harrumphed. "What do people do when they

get sad?"

"Cry?"

"No."

"They don't?"

"Well, yes," said Mr. Snickings, "but what *else* do they do?"

"Sulk?"

"They eat chocolate, you imbecile!"

"Oh, yes, that too, I suppose." Perkder then jolted as the revelation of what Mr. Snickings was saying knocked him upside the head. And that's when Perkder did something he rarely did. He frowned. "That's terrible."

"It's *not* terrible. It's profitable."

"Mr. Snickings, are you seriously asking me to make people sad so that they can go about buying more chocolate?"

"No," Finver said seriously, "I would never ask you to do such a thing."

"Good, because—"

"I'm *telling* you to do it! There ain't no asking going on from this side of the desk," he added while making a little swirling motion with his finger.

"Well, I won't do it, Mr. Snickings," Perkder said, crossing his arms. "People should be happy, not sad. I won't be a party to making people sad."

"I assumed that you'd say something stupid like that," Finver Snickings replied with a roll of his eyes, and then he did something *he* rarely did: he grinned. Then he reached into his desk and pulled out a piece of paper and three Halfly's chocolate bars. "Here's your final pay and some wrapped-happiness. Turn in your badge and locker key on your way out."

"You're firing me?" said Perkder with his mouth agape.

"Not so stupid after all, I see."

ORCMART

*G*rubby Longthumper knew his role on this mission. Keep an eye on Modacio and make sure that she kept to the plan and delivered the goods. He would also try to learn about this mysterious missing step that she had stated that the Zomboner Corporation had missed. Not that he'd planned on sharing that step with Teggins, of course. One didn't get to the highest point as a thief by sharing secrets, after all. Modacio had little choice in the matter of sharing that secret, assuming she wanted to stay alive, but Grubby didn't have a price on his head. His plan was to get the secret, see an accident befall Modacio, and claim ignorance while pulling in millions under the table.

The Ogre, Kone, had stayed quiet for most of the trip. He'd spent the majority of his time digging at his nose and studying whatever contents he was able to excavate. Grubby had nothing against Ogres as long as they were of the gruff variety. Unfortunately, Kone seemed to be more of the dumb type. The oaf had picked up Grubby once already, as was the norm with the dumber Ogres, but after a stern talking-to, he promised not to do it again.

"Why are we heading to Dogda?" asked Grubby as they arrived at the Civen Portal Station.

"There are only about five hundred known Zombies in the Underworld," answered Modacio. "Of those, the masses live in caves or in remote areas. Not many city dwellers."

"I know all this. Why Dogda?"

"Because a contact of mine says that a Zombie has been living there regular for the last two years."

Grubby wanted to question the sanity of that move, but then he thought about it. Dark Halflings called Dogda home, and Dark Halflings were rude, even if he did say so himself. They spoke their minds. If you were fat, they called you fat. If you were dumb, they called you dumb. If you stank and were rotting, they called you a Zombie. Now, if you were a Zombie, they just called a Zombie with the underlying assumption that you understood that they meant you stank and were rotting. When compared to any other place in the world of Ononokin, a Zombie would be called fewer things while living in Dogda.

"Pretty clever, actually," Grubby said with a smirk.

"I don't care if he is or isn't," Modacio said after entering in the coordinates on the portal for transportation to Dogda and got ready to engage the system. "I just want a piece of his flesh so that I can clear my name."

Bob slipped out the back of his tiny apartment. He never went out the front because that's where all his neighbors hung out. The Dark Halflings were livable, but the other races inhabiting his complex were cruel at best.

Climbing down the fire escape ladder, Bob gently padded to the ground with a wince. It was a risk every time he dropped from the ladder. Just a little to the left or a little to the right and he'd break an ankle or a knee. And if he fell over… well, that would be all she wrote for his hips.

Fortunately, he landed successfully and headed off into the night toward the grocery store.

～

"Der am a lot of little people here," Kone said with a giggle.

"Put them down," Modacio said, smacking Kone hard on his bicep.

"Ow!" Kone put an angry Dark Halfling down and rubbed his arm. "Why'd you hit me for?"

"Because you're an idiot, I'm guessing," said Grubby.

"He's not an idiot," Modacio said in Kone's defense. "He's just a little slow sometimes."

"Yeah," Kone said, looking angrily at Grubby. "I are just slow sometimes."

"My apologies," Grubby replied nonchalantly. "I had no idea you two were a couple."

Modacio rolled her eyes and pulled up her ePad while Grubby took a note about how he thought that Modacio and Kone were bedfellows. It had no actual bearing on the success of their mission, but he *did* say he'd report everything.

"A couple of what?" said Kone after a pause.

"So how are you planning to find this Zombie?" asked Grubby, ignoring the Ogre's question. "It's not like we're in a small city here."

"Look like a small city to me. Who da stupid one now?"

"You are," Grubby stated and then turned back to Modacio. "Well?"

"That's what I was just looking up. My contact says that our target has just entered Orcmart."

"What the hell does a Zombie need with Orcmart?" asked Grubby with a mean chuckle. "Did they start selling replacement thumbs or something?"

Bob walked into Orcmart as if he were just a normal, everyday customer. Fortunately, the average clientele at Orcmart was just a shade over the makings of a Zombie. On average, they were hygienically-challenged, poorly dressed, grotesquely overweight or disturbingly emaciated, and they sported the average IQ of a dust mite.

They were Bob's kind of people.

One of his favorite Undernet sites was PeopleOfOrcmart, after all. The pictures were so funny that Bob had to use caution when looking at them. The repercussions of a Zombie laughing too hard could cause all sorts of permanent facial damage, not to mention a dislocated lung.

He looked over his shopping list. It was the same stuff he'd always bought: bandages, cologne, and scented candles. Bob was in a constant battle with smells. The scented candles only lasted half their normal life when trying to combat the stench that he emanated, and the cologne burned his flesh like holy water on a Vampire.

As he approached the candle aisle, he noticed an Ogre was looking at him from over one of the shelves. Bob sighed as best as a Zombie could and then squared one of his shoulders—the other one never cooperated. He pressed on to the candle aisle.

Turning, he found a Human woman wearing a tight-fitting black outfit. She was gorgeous. To Bob, though—

someone who'd been a Zombie for many years and who hadn't felt the welcoming touch of a female form in all that time—he would consider a Troll with crossed eyes and a runny nose as acceptably attractive.

He backed away and waited for her to finish before he entered the aisle.

"It's okay," she said with a smile. "I'm not one of *those* people."

Bob attempted to blink, which was hard to do when one was without full eyelids. "Oh," he said back, surprised. "Thank you."

"My, uh, father was a Zombie," she said in a way that made Bob think that she was making that up...on a subconscious level, anyway. His conscious thoughts didn't care what she said as long as she kept talking. "I mean after he and my mom, well, you know." She stepped forward and put out her hand. It was gloved. "My name is Mod...uh...Maddy."

Bob looked at her hand and gingerly put his out. She gently shook it as he said, "I'm Bob."

"Bob? Odd name for a Human."

"Full name is Bobinguck Mermenhermen."

Just then an Orc came into the aisle and said gruffly, "Dis guy botherin' you, lady?"

Maddy turned and put a hand on her hip and started pointing at the Orc. "Not in the least, and it pains me to no end that people like you pick on him just because he's a Zombie."

"Uh," the Orc said, looking over at Bob, "I didn't know he was a Zombie, lady. I mean, I can smell it now and all, but to me all non-Orcs look alike."

"Oh, well, then—"

"I just seen this guy paddin' around in here a lot lately and he's got a no-good look about him. Maybe that's cause he's a Zombie?"

"Hey," Bob said, feeling a bit miffed.

"Well, he's just fine, thank you very much."

"Whatever you say, lady," the Orc replied with a shrug. "Just doin' my job."

"Sorry about that," Maddy said to Bob as the Orc walked away.

"I'm used to it."

Grubby had been standing in the next aisle listening to every word and jotting down a few notes.

Modacio was playing the guy well enough, though she had stumbled a bit at the start. It wasn't like it was all that difficult to fool a Zombie. Nobody paid them any attention, except to yell derogatory terms at them, so Modacio had a captive audience regardless of what she said.

Across the way, Kone was playing around with the stuffed animals. He was currently holding a fluffy green bunny while digging through his pockets, no doubt searching for a couple of coins.

"What are you doing?" whispered Grubby.

"Whut?" said Kone at full voice.

"Shhh! What are you doing?"

Kone scrunched up his face as if thinking very hard. Then he pointed at the bunny and held up the money.

"You should be paying attention over here," Grubby said, motioning toward the next aisle over.

"You fink dat guy wants a bunny?"

"Shhh! No, you dolt. I think that you need to put the bunny down and get ready in case something happens."

"Like whut?"

"Shhh! What if the guy runs away?"

"Him a Zombie," Kone said with a look that conveyed he thought Grubby was the stupid one in this conversation. "He ain't runnin' nowhere."

"Shhh! For the love of The Twelve! Shhh!"

"Why you keep shushin' me and den askin' me questions? How am I s'posed to answer questions if I gotta stay shushed?"

"Shhh!"

"You shhh! I'm buying dis bunny."

"I'll rip it to shreds, if you do."

Kone took two long strides across and picked up Grubby by the top of his head and looked squarely in his eyes. "You touch dis bunny and I punch you in da nose. You got dat?"

"Got it," grunted Grubby as the crushing force of Kone's fingers dug into his skull. "…and shhh."

Kone put Grubby back down and said, "Humph!" Then he walked toward the registers.

It would be a wonder if the Zombie hadn't overheard most of that conversation. Grubby could only hope that the rotter was too engaged talking with Modacio, which would make a lot of sense seeing that she was quite easy on the eyes.

Peeking through the shelves he found that they were no longer there. That could be fortunate or not, depending on one's perspective.

"Need help with something?" said a sultry voice, causing Grubby to jump nearly half is own height.

He turned around and found a Dark Halfling Vampiress standing there. Where Modacio was attractive, this one was a goddess. She was tall, by Dark Halfling standards, had long silver hair, piercing emerald eyes, ruby red lips, and she carried herself with attitude.

Grubby gulped.

"No, uh," he said, picking up the nearest box as if he'd intended to purchase it. "I just needed some..." He looked at the item he'd picked up and gulped again. "...Some, uh, feminine pads."

The worker looked him over. "You don't look like you'd need *feminine* products."

"Oh, no," he said with a silly laugh that did nothing but make him feel even sillier. "You see, it's *not* for me. It's for my, uh..." He didn't want to say "wife" or "girlfriend." Not that he had a chance with this girl or anything, but that wasn't the point. One never knew what women found attractive, so why tip his hand? "My...uh...cat."

"Your cat?" she said, crossing her arms.

"Yes, that's right. Mrs. Uh...Peebles. My cat. She has a, well, issue with urinating all the time."

"Sounds like you need pet diapers, then," she said, taking the box out of his hands and putting it back on the shelf. She then put a finger under his chin and pulled him along. "I'll show you where they are."

~

Ten minutes later Grubby darted out the Orcmart, feeling like an utter fool.

There was no doubt that Modacio had set him up by sending the Dark Halfling Vampire to distract him. As he thought about it, even the damned Ogre had been in on it. What self-respecting thief would *buy* a stuffed animal, after all? Then he thought about that and wondered what self-respecting *Ogre* would buy a stuffed bunny?

Regardless, this spelled certain doom for both Modacio and Kone. He knew they were in the city or at the portal.

One quick message from him to Teggins and they'd both be having tombstones carved.

"Where have you been?"

Grubby turned and saw Modacio sitting on one of the posts. Kone was petting the bunny. So they hadn't run away. That was surprising. And Kone had bought the stuffed animal. Even more surprising.

"Uh," he said, his confidence shaken ever so slightly.

"Because of you," Modacio said menacingly, "I had to let the Zombie go about his business."

"It couldn't be helped," Grubby said desperately. "I uh—"

Modacio leaned over and peeked into his shopping bag. "Oh," she said with a shocked look. "I'm sorry...I didn't know you had a problem."

"What him get?"

"Diapers."

"You poop yourself?"

"No, I did not poop myself," Grubby said, affronted.

"Now, Kone," said Modacio sternly, "what did we say about you having a filter?"

"Sorry."

Modacio smiled back at Grubby. "There's nothing to be ashamed about. Many people have issues like this."

Grubby was grimacing as he felt his ire rising.

"Like I said," he said through clenched teeth, "I don't have any problems. These are for my cat."

"You brought a cat?" said Kone excitedly.

"No, I didn't bring a cat!"

"Then why you got diapers for a cat?"

"Because they're not for a cat," explained Modacio. "Really, Grubby, you shouldn't feel bad about this. I've read a number of males at your age have problems with this. It's just nature's way of telling you that you're entering into a new era of life."

Grubby scowled and then threw the bag in the trash bin.

"I *don't* have a problem."

Modacio shrugged and said, "Hey, they're your clothes."

"That's right, they are...wait...seriously, I don't have any problems with that!"

"Okay," Modacio replied as she got up and started heading down the street.

Grubby grunted, deciding to leave this part out of his notes. "Where are we going?"

Modacio pointed down the road. In the distance was the limping form of a Zombie turning a corner.

"I was hoping to have taken him sooner, but I didn't know where you were."

"Oh."

"It's okay," she added gently. "I didn't know about your *not-a-problem* problem."

"Yeah," Kone sat, patting Grubby on the head.

Grubby slapped away the Ogre's hand.

"Can we just get this Zombie and quit talking about this...please?"

COULD YOU GIVE US A HAND?

*B*ob hadn't felt this good in years.

There was just something about a lady talking to you and not telling you how bad you smelled or what a disgrace you were that brought out the best in your mood. It wasn't like he'd gotten her TalkyThingy number or anything. There was only so much a Zombie could hope for, after all. But she'd *talked* to him. She'd even kept talking to him for a little while outside of the Orcmart before he'd headed back to his apartment.

And now he was taking a nice gingerly pace while attempting to whistle a happy tune. It sounded like the sucking of a chest wound to his ears, but in his head it was a song about daisies and blue skies.

There were only a couple more blocks to go before he turned into the back alley that marked his way of entering his apartment.

He never went this way on weekends because the teenagers hung around the dumpsters and threw stuff at him, assuming they were in a good mood. Bob didn't even want to think about the things they did to him when they were feeling antsy. During the week, though, he was careful to stick to the back alleys in order to avoid the parents of those teenagers doing the same things to him if he came in the front way. At this hour, it wasn't likely anyone would bother him, anyway.

Schlop.

Bob heard a schlopping sound and stopped to make sure none of his body parts had fallen off. It happened from time to time. All part of being a Zombie.

Nothing was out of place, so he continued on in his shuffling way, picking up that daisy-blue-sky tune again in his head.

Schlop schlop.

Bob stopped and glanced back.

He saw a towering figure about half a block behind him. At that size it was either an Orc or an Ogre. Not even Trolls got that big, and there weren't any Giants or Gorgans living in these parts. Whatever it was, it had started milling about as if nothing were going on.

If Bob'd had a useful heart, he assumed that it would have been beating frantically at the moment.

He spun back and picked up his pace a bit. This took a lot of focus since one wrong move would have cost him a foot.

Schlop schlop schlop.

The footsteps were catching up now.

Bob wasn't about to look back because, in his estimation, looking forward got you where you wanted to be faster. As he turned the corner, he carefully pulled over one of the empty trashcans to hopefully buy himself some more time.

Schlop schlop schlop bang bing bong thud..."Ouch!"

It wasn't much, but it was enough.

He reached the ladder that led up to his apartment and

carefully started to pull himself up. Getting to the third rung, he felt a giant hand grab his ankle.

"Hello there," said a familiar voice.

Bob looked down and saw Maddy standing to the side. Next to her was a Dark Halfling. Glancing down he saw the Ogre that obviously had been following him. It was holding his leg.

"Maddy?"

"Sure," she said with a shrug and a fake grin.

"What's going on?"

"Well," she said, crossing her arms, "we were hoping you could…give us a hand."

"Or a foot," pointed out the Dark Halfling.

"True," Maddy said with a half-nod. "A foot would do fine, too."

"What are you talking about?"

"Bob, Bob, Bob," said Maddy as she swirled her boot around in a puddle of water. "Did you honestly think someone that looked like me would truly care about the likes of you?"

"But, you treated me so kindly."

"She set you up, you dimwit," said the Dark Halfling. "Now give us a chunk of your flesh willingly or our pal here will just rip off a piece."

Bob turned back to the Ogre, who said, "Hello" in a sing-song way.

"Why do you want my flesh?"

"We makin' erech…erect…no, dat's not it…boner pills!"

"Shut up, you blockhead!"

"Dat not my name, Grubby. My name is Kone and you knows dis already."

"You're a horrible person," Bob said suddenly, turning back to the woman. "I'll bet your name isn't even Maddy."

"You right, mister. Dat not her name. It Modacio."

"Idiot!"

"No, it Modacio. I known her longer den you, Grubby."

"*You* are the idiot," the one called Grubby said.

"I am not," said the Ogre, letting go of Bob's ankle. "I'm just slow. We already talk about dis."

Bob took the moment to reach up to the next rung and pull with all his might. That turned out to be a mistake because his hand couldn't handle the pressure. With a crunching pop, it came off at the wrist and dropped to the street below.

It didn't hurt. When things fell off they never hurt. They were just gone.

"Fanks, mister," Kone said with a smile as he picked up the hand and put it in a plastic case. "See," Kone said to the other two, "I told ya all ya gotsta do is ask. And you say *I'm* da dumb one."

"Bye bye, Bob," Maddy or Modacio or whoever the hell she really was said with a little cutesy wave.

"Give me back my hand!" he cried, but they ignored him and kept walking down the street.

How could she? How could *anyone* be so cruel? And how the hell was he supposed to get up or down the ladder now that he only had one hand and it was his bad hand?

No. No. No! There was no way he was going to let this happen. It was horrible enough to have to go through life in a constant state of advanced decay. Bob wasn't about to do it with his hand missing, too. Sure, he could find a replacement, but dammit…that was *his* hand, and he wanted it back.

He tried to slide down a single rung of the ladder. It felt like he was going to make it until his ankle gave out and he dropped straight down onto the street below, snapping his thigh bone in the process.

Again, there was no pain, but Bob well understood that he was not going to be able to walk or get up the ladder, and there was no chance he'd catch up to the thieves…not that he could have done anything to get his hand back from them anyway.

So he just lay there for a while, trying to cry while thinking about what to do. Crying was just as pointless as most anything else that a regular person would take for granted. Regardless, he sure as hell wasn't smiling.

Bob only had one friend that he could count on, but he was two long blocks away and he would be sound asleep at this time of the night. He could call Dr. Mozatto, but the psychiatrist would just tell him to go to the emergency room. The ER would just tell him to go jump in a lake. The fish in that lake would tell him to choose some other lake to jump into.

Seeing no other real options, he decided that a friend was a friend whether it was in the morning or in the middle of the night, so he started to drag himself toward the home of Perkder Stonepebble.

MAKESHIFT PORTAL

*M*odacio, Kone, and Grubby cut through the alleys until they reached the field that lay to the west of Halfly's Park. It was the only place that was dark and wooded enough to give them a chance to launch the makeshift portal before anyone from Portal Authority could catch them.

"This is illegal, you know," Grubby said as they pushed through the trees.

"Isn't most everything we do?" answered Modacio.

"Well, yeah, but I mean this is differently illegal."

"What difference does it make?"

Grubby felt the thwack of tiny branches barraging his cheeks as Kone's massive legs pushed through the brush ahead of him.

"Getting caught in the Underworld for theft lands you in the clink for a year, maybe two, and that's only if you've got a record. Taking an underground transport to the Upperworld, though, well, that'll get you a minimum of twenty years and a full cavity search every time you want to travel the legal portals from that point on!"

"Well, little man," Modacio retorted as they continued pushing their way through, "this wasn't the original plan. I was going to drop whatever body part I could snag into a sealed container and go on up to the Upperworld on my own. Being that I'm Human, I wouldn't have much problem getting through."

"They don't let—"

"What, Zombie parts through the scanners? I know all about that. But imagine me all dressed up in a sad dress, with a sad face, explaining that I had the only remaining part of my ever-dying husband in that container. His poor head was crushed in an industrial accident, mind you, thus relegating his ever-dying situation into a more permanent finally-dead one. And I was distraughtly taking it to Flaymtahk Island so that I could burn his final remains into infinity."

"Diabolical," said Grubby in amazement.

"I even had an official-looking death certificate drawn up, which cost me a few coins, by the way."

"So why can't we just do that, then?"

"Because now I've got you and Kone tagging along," she replied and then grunted as she kicked a branch out of the way. "Besides the obvious fact that you're a Dark Halfling and he's an Ogre, neither of which are allowed into the Upperworld without a VISA, it would also make my story a little less believable if I tried to pass you two off as family."

"Halflings are allowed up."

"Not the Dark kind, little man."

"I could just say I was caught out in the sun."

"And turned an almost transparent shade of blue? I don't think anyone would buy that. Halflings of the non-Dark variety turn a shade of red when they've been out in the sun too long."

"Makeup, then."

"That would probably work," Modacio conceded, "but that wouldn't do Kone any good, and since your boss made it quite clear that *you* were to join this exciting adventure to keep tabs on me, I decided it only fair to include Kone so that he can keep tabs on you."

"Who's keeping tabs on him?" asked Grubby with a hiss.

"I are tabbing myself!"

"Now," Modacio said as she paused to catch her breath, "I'll happily stop this route and go with my original plan if you want to sit around with Kone and wait for my eminent return."

"Not going to happen," said Grubby, realizing that the transportable portal that Teggins had provided the coordinates of would signal the union boss once it had fired off. If it didn't fire off, then Teggins would get suspicious and Grubby had no intention of becoming someone with whom the union decided to examine under a microscope. "I'm just saying that if we get caught it's going to be a rough future for us all."

"Then I guess we'd best not get caught," Modacio stated as she pushed back into the trees.

"Yeah, dat's a good plan. I not like gettin' caught. Always troubles when dat happens."

Grubby leaned forward and put his elbows up to ward off as much of the whipping sticks as he could. Fortunately, he was wearing his thick leather jacket with the long sleeves. His old ma had given it to him before he'd left the nest. Well, not exactly *given* it to him. It was more that his ma just gave him the stink eye without saying anything as Grubby'd swiped the jacket from his pa's closet. The fact was that his ma liked Grubby's pa a fair bit less than she disliked Grubby.

Fifteen minutes later, they entered a small clearing where the moonlight broke neatly through the trees, bathing the grass with its light. The chittering of insects amplified since the sound of Kone plodding through the forest had died down.

One of the good things about being a Dark Halfling, and there were many, was the ability to see clearly in even the darkest of nights. With the moon lifting the darkness slightly, it was almost as clear as day to Grubby.

He checked the area while the other two set to digging up the box that contained the portal and began piecing it together.

"No, Kone," Modacio was saying, "you don't put that end in the ground. If you do that we won't be able to press the buttons."

"Dat makes sense, I guess."

"I'll tell you what," she continued, "you hold that heavy piece there and I'll attach the wiring and get us going."

Something smelled funny about the area. Grubby couldn't quite make out what it was. Mostly because it was a mixture of smells. Grass, pollen, bark, bushes, Modacio, Kone—a lot of Kone, actually…talk about someone that could use a two-hour dip in a large soapy lake. But there was something else. Oil? Flint maybe? Feathers, definitely. That could just have been birds. There was also the scent of refined woods.

"Wait," he said, scooting over to Modacio and Kone.

"We're almost ready," Modacio said. "Just relax."

"Something's wrong."

"Yeah, you in da way, dat's what."

"I'm growing tired of you, you overgrown chump," Grubby said, pulling himself to his full height and poking a pointed finger at Kone's knee.

"At least somefin' about you is growin'."

"Okay, you two," Modacio said. "Stop it already. I swear, you're worse than children!"

"He started it."

"Nuh-uh! Him did!"

"Grubby," Modacio said as she finished twisting two wires together, "you said that something was wrong?"

"Oh, right, yeah, I smell something funny."

"Prolly yer upper lip."

"That's it—"

Grubby wrapped himself around Kone's leg and took to biting him on the quadriceps.

"Ouch! What him bitin' me for?"

Suddenly, Grubby wondered if this had been such a wise move. He felt Kone's enormous hands grab him from both sides. Then he felt a whoosh of air as he was launched straight upward toward the moon.

It had happened so fast that Grubby didn't feel the panic set in until gravity began to take its hold again.

Looking down, the Dark Halfling saw the tops of the trees coming back toward him. He wanted to scream, but he was in shock. Still, as he cannoned down toward Kone, he saw a stream of lights about a half mile away from their position and they were closing fast.

"...catch him or we'll both be hunted by the damn union," Modacio was yelling as Grubby saw the ground speedily approaching.

Kone groaned and reached out.

The wind was knocked completely out of Grubby, but he managed to say, "They're coming! Must...hurry!"

He heard shouts of "Over there!" and "Get them!" as the world slowly faded away.

HELP FROM A FRIEND

*P*erkder Stonepebble wobbled down the street toward his house as he drunkenly wondered what he was going to do next.

Working at Halfly's Park had been one of the grandest things he'd ever done. It gave him the creative outlet to dance around, act silly, dress up in various costumes, and make people happy. Other than the circus, which was full of, well, circus-freaks, there were few options that allowed him to be himself. Yes, he had the *CosPlay Posse*, and it was a fantastic group, but it wasn't a job, per se. Though, he thought, with a bit of effort, maybe it could be.

The world was rarely dreary to someone like Perkder. His was a vision that was covered with rose-inlaid glasses. Seeing the world in pastels made it difficult to fall into the gray of life.

A song came to him as he sloshed through the puddles while a steady drizzle pattered upon his wide-brimmed hat.

And a ho-ho-ho

And a way we go
Dressing up in the valley of the Lappy Dappy Doh
Looking like a bunch of fools with our robes flowing low
And a way we go
And a ho-ho-ho!

"Shut up, you idiot," yelled a gruff voice from one of the buildings to Perkder's left. "People are trying to sleep up here!"

"Sorry," Perkder called back with a wave.

"It's two in the morning, you daft Dwarf!"

"Right," Perkder said, pointing. "My apologeeez."

Windows slammed shut, putting an exclamation point on the feelings of those living nearby.

Perkder sang again, but this time much more quietly as he plodded along.

Little dream barrister alone in the night
Bringing up the bunnies and puppies and—Bob?

Perkder stopped for a second, blinking while trying to regain his bearings. There was someone propped up against the railing that led up to Perkder's townhouse. It sure looked like Bob.

"Bob?"

"Yeah," Bob replied in his husky voice.

Perkder went to rush to his friend, but the world was still moving in such a way that made him more carefully tread.

"You...you...you okay?"

"No," stated Bob, holding up his arm. "They took my

hand, Perkder. The bastards took my hand."

"Who...*hic*...took your hand?"

"Oh, I've got their names," Bob said ominously. "I've got them and I'm planning to get my hand back. You can bet your butt on that."

"Good," Perkder said and then burped. "Sorry. Why are...*hic*...are you here?"

"I need your help, Perkder."

"My...*hic*...help?"

~

It had taken an hour for Perkder to sober up enough to be somewhat levelheaded.

During his wait, Bob had successfully pulled himself onto one of the chairs that Perkder had offered. That was one of the nice things about Perkder—he saw the truth behind Bob's situation, not the myths and legends. Fact was that there were many nice things about his Dwarfish friend.

"Sorry you lost your job," Bob said sadly.

"Me too, Bob," Perkder replied while drinking another cup of HighCaff tea. "I really liked that job." He then shrugged and added, "But I'm a firm believer that things happen for a reason."

"But why does it always happen to the good ones?"

"True," Perkder said with a solemn nod. "True."

The Dwarf set the cup down and took a deep breath. Bob missed the ability to really take a deep breath and give a full sigh. If he'd done that now, his lung would burst. Not that it mattered, since he was effectively dead anyway, but it was the point of the thing.

"So," Perkder said, leaning forward, "you said that there were three of them, right?"

Bob nodded. "A Human female, a Dark Halfling, and an Ogre."

"Mean or dumb?"

"Hmmm?"

"The Ogre," Perkder clarified. "Was he the mean type or the dumb type."

"I didn't really talk to him that much, but he seemed kind of childlike to me."

"Dumb type, then," Perkder said. "That's a good thing. You don't want to mess with mean Ogres."

"I don't want to mess with any Ogres," admitted Bob. "I just want my hand back."

"You know, there are a lot of prosthetic devices on the market these days that are pretty high-tech."

"They're going to make boner medication out of my limb, Perkder."

"I know, I know…I'm just saying…" Perkder trailed off for a second. "Okay, let's look this up and see what they've got to do."

Perkder pulled up his machine and got on the UnderNet. He was zipping around using Gnoogle and Gnomepedia, until he finally landed on a number of articles related to the use of Zombie parts and medication.

"Here it is," Perkder said. "Looks like they're going to the Upperworld. They're going to Flaymtahk Island. Ever heard of it?"

"No."

"It's basically an island just beyond the northern tip of the Upperworld. It's on the west side of the continent. Lots of volcanoes and lava and such. Hot place."

"Sounds like it."

"Yeah," Perkder said and then ran his finger across the screen. "Says here that they'll have to take your hand and put it in the correct lava pit while using an iron ladle. It'll melt, leaving a greenish liquid behind. If they take that and mix it with the proper ingredients, they'll be able to make erection medication...or tons of other things, of course."

"I thought this had already been tried, though?"

"It has been. A few times, actually. According to this there are three types of lava pits that are available. One of them will turn the flesh properly; one of them has no actual evidence of what it will do, but it's assumed nothing; and the last of them will cause a Caklactic Rift, instantly killing the original owner of the flesh."

They looked at each other momentarily. Perkder's eyes were wide, Bob's were lidless.

"So if they get the wrong one, it'll kill me?"

"That's what it says."

"Hmmm," Bob said, thinking that it was better than "living" the rest of his days as a Zombie.

"I know what you're thinking, Bob," said Perkder, waving his finger, "but to go down in history as having died due to an erection medication attempt is pretty pathetic."

Bob did the only kind of sigh he could, which sounded more like a wet hiss.

"Good thing I got fired, I suppose," Perkder said, standing up and smiling broadly. "Otherwise, how could I help you get your hand back? Like I said, Bob, I believe that things always happen for a reason."

"You're really going to help me?"

"Of course! I can't leave a friend of mine to die simply because it's a bit inconvenient. Now, we have work to do. They're not just going to let a Dwarf and a Zombie into the Upperworld, you know? We'll need to..."—his eyes sparkled for a moment—"...dress up."

"Hmmm," said Bob again.

LESANG

*T*he town of Lesang was known as *the* place to be, assuming you were wealthy.

All the rich and famous either had a summer cottage there or they lived there full time, especially after retirement. Many of the houses were extravagant, to say the least. The amount of gold adornments alone could pay off the national debt of most countries.

One would expect the residents of Lesang to be uppity, snobbish, and egotistical...and one would be correct. However, these were a people who prided themselves on being better than everyone else, and that meant that each felt it their personal obligation to point out to those who were less fortunate that they, the less fortunate, were, in fact, less fortunate.

An interesting psychological oddity, to anyone who saw beyond the plethora of normal oddities, was that they loved to entertain interesting races. This was especially true of Underworld races.

For the most part, the Underworld was a thing of legend to those who lived in the Upperworld. But there were a few in certain stations—such as kings, soldiers, and wizards—who knew the truth. The wealthy had a way of knowing things too, since kings and wizards often fraternized with people entrenched with insane amounts of money.

The races from the Underworld that Lesangians loved were Vampires, Zombies, Halflings, Ogres (the dumb kind), and Werewolves. They weren't very fond of Underworld Humans, Dwarfs, Dark Halflings, Orcs, Ogres (the mean kind), or Trolls. To be fair, people of wealth in the Upperworld *did* like to visit Troll-run hotels and casinos in the Underworld, but that was a different story altogether.

Sadly, neither Modacio, Grubby, or Kone knew about this oddity that the wealthy had, so when their portal finished discharging them directly next to a security station at the top of a hill overlooking the seaport area of Lesang, both Modacio and Grubby were quickly taken into custody. Kone, on the other hand, was just asked to wait for a few minutes.

"Where are you taking us?" asked Modacio gruffly.

"Down to the cells, miss," the guard cordially replied.

Grubby grunted, looking like he was still trying to get the cobwebs cleared after being knocked out. He said, "We've done nothing wrong and you know it."

"Not for me to say, sir. I just know that there was an unauthorized access to the area from the Underworld." Then he pointed at each of them in turn, whispering, "You're a Human and you're a Dark Halfling, and that—"

"How do you know I'm not a regular Halfling?" Grubby said with a sneer.

"You got a blue tint about you," whispered the guard, apparently wanting to make sure the other prisoners didn't hear him. Then he turned to open one of the cell doors, motioning them inside. "We get training on these things. Bottom line is that you two are unwanted folk in this area."

"But you'll let an Ogre run free?" asked Modacio with a look of surprise, keeping her voice low as well.

"Only the dumb ones, miss, and we'll have a guard with him at all times, too, of course."

"He's not dumb," Modacio replied, sticking up for her business partner.

"Yes, he is," argued Grubby. "Even this guy knows that."

The guard nodded, smiling. "We'll have someone come down to talk to you in the morning." He then locked the door and padded away.

"If Kone is so dumb," said Modacio haughtily as she watched the guard depart, "why is he free to roam the streets while we're stuck in jail?"

Grubby hopped up on one of the metal benches. "Dumb ain't the same thing as lucky."

"You think being born an Ogre is lucky?"

"At the moment I do," Grubby answered while putting his head in his hands.

~

Kone wasn't sure what to do.

He'd never been to the Upperworld before and this place had a look to it that spelled someone of his nature wouldn't be welcomed. But the security guard had been really nice to him. Of course he'd been nice to Modacio and that little weasel, Grubby, too, but they'd been arrested where Kone was free, sort of.

"But I never get to do anything!" complained a young guard as he walked out of the building with an older guard.

"Enough of your whining, Johnson," stated the older guard. "It's Bledstone's turn to act as chaperon and that's that."

57

"His turn?" said Johnson, looking steamed. "He's the one that got to go with Miss Wedlow just the other day to the market. And I've had to do day shift three times this week. He's not had to do it once."

"Well, Mr. Picky," said the older guard with a grunt, "I guess we'll just have to look over the schedule again to make sure that *you* are kept happy."

That quieted Johnson for long enough that the older guy had time to walk away.

"What am I supposed to do?" Kone asked Johnson.

"Not much to do in the middle of the night around here," Johnson said with a bit of a shrug. "I'm sure there are some parties down on the west side pier. Usually are, anyway. You could head over there and have some fun."

"Hmmm," said Kone, digging into his ear, "I fink Modacio would get mad at me if I done that."

"She won't even know," the guard pointed out, rocking on his heels. "Truth is that she'll probably be stuck in that cell with her little friend for at least a couple of days. That's how long it'll take to get them properly transfered back to the Underworld. One of the mayor's aides just has to get the ball rolling, is all."

"Oh," said Kone forlornly. "Dat will put dem in a bunch of trouble."

"They're definitely looking at jail time in the Underworld. At least, assuming all the rumors I've heard are true."

"Dey are," said Kone. "I don't wanna go ter no jail, mister."

The guard smiled. "Worry not about that, my friend. You are of a different sort than your two friends. You'll be taken care of nicely, and securely returned home whenever you wish it."

"Really? Why?"

"Let's just say that the folks around here find you people fascinating."

Kone grimaced and squinted at the guard. "What do you mean, *you people?*"

"Uh…Underworlders."

"My friends is from der, too," said Kone. "I don't fink dat's what you meaned."

"Johnson," called out another guard from inside the booth, "I'll take it from here."

"Right," said Johnson as if the world had just given him a gift, which, for all intents and purposes, it had. "Sorry, sir," he said hurriedly to Kone. "I have to run."

Kone watched the little man disappear into the building. Then he sighed and reached into his sack and pet the stuffed bunny that he'd purchased at Orcmart.

Another guard came out. He was larger than the others, and he looked strong for a Human. Kone could obviously still snap him in two, if the need arose, but hopefully that wouldn't be necessary. Right behind him followed a smaller man who was wearing a red robe that matched his pointy red beard. He looked a little bit like a Human-sized Gnome.

"Name is Bledstone," said the guard, putting out his hand.

Kone carefully shook the hand and said, "Kone."

"This is Master Wizard Redler."

"Hoopdee dah!" said the wizard as if presenting himself to an audience of thousands.

Kone looked at Bledstone, who merely shrugged. "Never quite know, to be honest."

"Him said just saying hello," Kone stated.

"You can understand him?"

"I guess."

"Interesting. Well, he's here to cast a spell on you so that the commoners won't know you're an Ogre."

"What are dat?"

"An Ogre? Shouldn't you already know—"

"No, not that. What a spell?"

"Oh, right! I forgot that you guys in the Underworld don't really keep up on things like this. Like I said before, Mr. Redler there is a wizard."

Kone had heard him the first time, but he wasn't sure what a wizard was. The word had sounded familiar, but Kone was having trouble placing its origin. He thought back to the stories that he'd heard about the Upperworld while growing up. They had those guys that dressed up in all silver who carried long sticks. Always trying to poke each other off their horses. No, those were Knights. There were those guys that wore crowns on their heads that ruled with an iron fist. He snapped his fingers. Kings! That's what those guys were called. Then a thought popped into his brain. Weren't wizards the ones that carried around little sticks around with them? Yeah, that's right. They wore robes, just like the Redler guy was wearing, too. Some of them had on hats with a big point on them. But what was it that they actually did for a living? And then it hit him. Kone looked up, his mouth dropping open. He felt a sudden sense of panic. "Magic?"

"Don't worry," Bledstone said, patting Kone on the shoulder. "It's nothing. I see him do it all the time. Never once has anyone been bothered by it."

"But magic is da fings of evil!"

"Loodle da pop?"

They both looked questioningly at the wizard.

Then, Bledstone took a breath and looked at Kone. "You don't have to let him do it, if you don't want, but that just means we'll be sitting here the entire night instead of hitting a party."

Kone liked parties. "There gonna be music there?"

"Oh yeah," said Bledstone with glee. "Loud music, too."

"I like music." Kone picked his nose again. "Okay," he said after some thought, "how do dis magic stuff work?"

"I can't answer that," said Bledstone. "I'm not a wizard. But I do know that all the wealthy people on the island, and all the guards, and a select few others, wear special rings that show through the magic spells." Bledstone showed his ring. It was thin and silver with a tiny blue stone in the middle. "Everyone that has one of these on will see you as you really are. All the others will see you as, well, whatever Mr. Redler makes them see."

Kone gulped. "It gonna hurt?"

"Peddle, peddle, peddle," said Master Wizard Redler with a shake of his head.

"Okay." Kone gulped, but there was something about the wizard that made him feel comfortable. "I s'pose you can do dat magic stuff, den."

The wizard smiled and nodded. He started waving his arms about while chanting something that sounded even more like gibberish than his normal speech. Little flecks of light began to form at his fingers until finally he thrust his hands toward Kone, releasing a torrent of light while the Ogre screeched in fear.

Then, it was over.

Kone hadn't felt a thing. He looked himself over and didn't notice anything different either. Maybe it didn't work?

"I don't see nuffin'," he said to Bledstone.

"That's because of two things," replied Bledstone. "First, you're the one that the spell was cast upon, so you won't see it. Second, you're an Underworlder."

"Why do dat matter?"

"Well, imagine a bunch of Underworlders came up, right? The wizard casts spells on them all, yeah? Now, we either have to make rings for all of them or we have to set it up so that they, being Underworlders themselves and, thus, are used to seeing other Underworlders, aren't fooled by the spell."

"Ah," said Kone with a furrow of his brow. "Dat makes sense. But what do I look like?"

Master Wizard Redler grabbed Kone's wrist and pulled him over to a section of the building that had metal walls. It wasn't a perfect mirror, but Redler cast another spell that lit things up nicely enough that Kone could see his reflection.

"I look like I always look," said Kone.

"Oooh, der!" the wizard cast another spell on the wall and Kone saw himself as a tall, lanky Human with long black hair.

"Dat's me?"

"That's what people see when they see you," said Bledstone. "Assuming they don't have a ring."

Kone regarded his new look and found he kind of liked it. Being an Ogre wasn't always what it was cracked up to be, after all. To look somewhat normal, like the visage that the wizard had turned him into, would be nice sometimes.

After a few moments, the wizard looked at his wrist, bowed and said, "Keedly umpah." Then he walked away.

"Right," said Bledstone to Kone. "Well, you ready to party?"

With one last look at the facade of his reflection, Kone smiled and said, "Yep."

The guard looked relieved. "Excellent. Follow me!"

SECURITY CHECKPOINT

ou sure this is going to work?" asked Bob as he looked himself over in the mirror. Perkder had dressed him up in a flashy suit that he wouldn't have been caught, well, dead in were he not a Zombie. Being that he was a Zombie, and, again, dead, sort of, he thought that the suit was actually an improvement over his normal look. Bob did kind of like the top hat, too. It was a deep purple with a thick black band at its base. But, still…"I look like a pimp."

"Excellent! That's what I was going for."

"Why?"

"You'll see in a minute," said Perkder as he finished putting gobs of makeup on Bob's face. "Good enough. Let me get dressed and we'll get out of here."

Perkder hopped off the chair he'd been standing on and scooted toward his wardrobe room. Bob had never seen so many outfits in one place. Everything from full animal costumes to things Bob didn't even want to wonder about.

"How are we going to get to this island, anyway?" he called out as best he could.

"Going through Lesang," Perkder replied, grunting.

"But Civen Station doesn't go there."

"Yergarn," said Perkder. "Have to go through Yergarn."

"Ugh," Bob said with a frown. "That means multiple stops."

"Not anymore," Perkder said. "Dogda now has a direct route to Yergarn. Been there for about three months now."

Bob hadn't known that, but Bob wasn't one to do much traveling.

"Oh, well, that's good, at least."

"Yep."

"But aren't there still issues with our kind getting into the Upperworld? It's not like we have a passport or anything."

"We just have to pass as Human," Perkder said, after which followed a crashing sound. "I'm okay. Just fell down trying to pull up these knickers."

"Good," Bob said, though he hadn't really been worried. Dwarfs, unlike Zombies—unless they were Zombie Dwarfs, obviously—were resilient folk. "So, I will *barely* pass as a Human, Perkder. One whiff of me and they'll be suspicious. But what about you?"

And that's when Perkder walked out of the wardrobe room. He was wearing a little pink dress, white stockings, ruby red shoes, a white sweater, elbow-length pink gloves, a blond wig, and a smile.

"Ta-da!"

"Uh…" Bob said, not knowing what else to say. "Please tell me you're not supposed to be my wife?"

"What?" said Perkder, scrunching up his nose. "No, of course not. I wouldn't marry a pimp!"

Bob then looked over his own outfit again and groaned. "So you're one of my…um…bitches?"

"No, I'm your daughter!"

"Oh, right," said Bob with a gentle nod. "That makes *much* more sense."

"I heard your sarcasm there, Bob. You really have to work on your happiness."

"I'll do that. Listen, don't you think we're going to look kind of suspicious?"

"Why? We're just a father and his ten-year-old daughter heading up to Lesang to visit relatives."

"Or, more accurately, we're a pimp and a young, um, girl."

"Fine, I'll take off the chains around your neck so you look less like a pimp."

"I'm sure that minor change will help, yes," Bob said with a cough. "But how, exactly, am I going to explain my daughter's beard?"

"Hmmm. Good point. I forget that Human females aren't graced with facial hair."

"Some are," noted Bob, "but I doubt that they consider it a blessing."

"You Humans are an odd folk."

Bob wasn't about to argue that point. To be fair, though, he was currently looking at a stocky Dwarf with a neatly trimmed beard who was dressed up like a child's doll.

"Anyway," said Perkder, "we'll just tell them that I've forgotten to shave."

"Right," said Bob, wondering how Perkder's brain really worked. "I'm sure they'll buy that, especially since they, too, know that Human females aren't privy to all that facial hair."

"Exactly. Now, we should get going while it's still the middle of the night. The station will be emptier and the night crews are generally less particular."

Bob doubted the logic of that statement. From his

perspective, going to Yergarn when it was packed full gave them a chance to be pushed through the process without much fuss. If things were slow, then they'd have more time to be questioned.

It's not like it really mattered all that much, anyway. If they got through, great; if not, then Bob's hand would either turn into a bottle of boner medication or the thieves would get the wrong type of lava and he'd die. *Really* die.

He'd struggled back and forth on that latter point. On the one hand, he'd never had the guts to take his own life in any permanent kind of way. Dr. Mozatto had often pointed out that Bob was too chicken to be a serious suicide risk. On the other hand—which he noted he no longer had—if the thieves wound up ending his life, then the pain and suffering would cease. It wasn't like he contributed anything to the world these days, anyway, unless you considered it contributive that his situation provided bullies with an easy target, or you took into account the current use of his body parts to manufacture medication, of course.

"I see what you're thinking, Bob," said Perkder with a shake of his head. "If it'll make you happy for me to shave, I'll shave."

The Dwarf was about to risk his personal station and everything in order to help Bob get his hand back. Why would he do that? What was in it for him?

"Why are you doing this, Perkder?"

"Shaving? Well, I'd rather not, truth be told."

"No, helping me. Why are you helping me?"

Perkder grimaced and quickly tilted his head. "That's what friends do, Bob. Good times and bad times. I'll be on your side forever more. That's what friends are for…hmmm, reminds me of a song."

And that's when Bob realized that there was at least one person in this Twelve-forsaken world that actually gave a damn about him. He had a friend in Perkder. A real friend. If nothing else, that proved that Bob had at least enough worth to try and save himself.

"No," he said finally, sitting up a little straighter in his chair, "don't shave. If those guards give me any trouble about my...daughter's facial hair issue, well, I'll just have to give them a verbal lashing."

"There you go, Bob," said Perkder with a wide grin, smacking Bob friendly-like on the back, causing the Zombie's shoulder to crunch and pivot awkwardly. "Oh, sorry," said Perkder as he pulled the shoulder back into place.

～

Residents of the Underworld were free to travel anywhere along the portal system as long as they stayed in the Underworld. There were exceptions to this rule, of course. Certain people, such as criminal, were banned from arriving at some destinations, and one *could* travel to the Upperworld if they were either granted rights via ambassadorship, special allowance like a travel VISA, or if they happened to actually live there.

This meant that getting to Yergarn Station from Dogda's base portal wasn't a problem for Bob and Perkder, even if they did get a number of odd looks along the way. The problem was going to be getting through security and into Lesang.

"Now what?" asked Bob as they stood before the security screening station to the portals that led to the Upperworld.

"We walk up there confidently," said Perkder, and then he

paused. "Well, *you* walk up there confidently. I'm going to skip up there."

"Skip?"

"Yeah, have to make it believable and all."

"Oh, right."

"Then you just tell them that you've been down here visiting and you're ready to return home to Lesang."

"And you think they'll buy that?"

Perkder shrugged. "If they don't, we'll figure something out." He scratched his beard and squinted. "That guard looks really familiar."

"So?"

"Just hate it when I can't place someone," said Perkder, grimacing.

They started to move when Bob stopped the Dwarf. "Wait a second. Isn't there another station we could go to that doesn't have all this security? I thought Aopow Station was more relaxed, no?"

"It is, but we'd still have to deal with officials on the other side."

"Ah," said Bob, nodding. "Won't we have to deal with them anyway?"

"Yep," said Perkder, and then he started skipping. "Let's go."

Bob did his weak sigh and carefully walked up to the security guard.

"Nice outfit," said the guard, sounding genuine.

"Oh, uh, thanks," Bob replied.

"Name?"

"Bob."

"Just Bob?"

"Bobinguck Mermenhermen."

"Seriously?" said the guard with his eyebrows raised.

"Is that a problem?" answered Bob in his raspy voice.

"Only in that I can't spell it."

Bob spelled his name slowly for the guard as Perkder kept jumping around.

"Right," said the guard with a curt smile. "Now, where is it that you and the Dwarf are going?"

"He's not a Dwarf," Bob said. "He's my daughter."

"*He's* your daughter?"

"She," Bob said, correcting himself. "*She* is my daughter."

"Uh-huh," the guard said, glancing over at Perkder. "My apologies to the little…girl. So, where are you and your *daughter* headed this night?"

"Back home to Lesang."

The guard looked up from the papers. "Lesang? That's in the Upperworld."

Bob kept quiet.

"Do you have permission to go to the Upperworld, Mr. Mermenhermen?"

"I come from the Upperworld," Bob replied tightly.

"Oh, I see," said the guard, leaning back and crossing his arms. "You're from the Upperworld," he added with a nod. "You and your daughter, there."

"Right."

"The one with the beard."

Bob leaned in and whispered, "She suffers from a case of Follicle Formation. It's a rare and untreatable disease, except with razors and shaving cream, obviously. She's very sensitive about it."

"I would imagine so," said the guard, looking unconvinced. "Funny thing that I've never heard of Follicle Formation disease."

"It's rare," Bob stated.

"Must be. You see I'm only doing the guard thing part-time while I'm in school for medicine, and we've just recently covered all of the various diseases. I got an *A* on the exam and everything. One hundred percent correct. We studied hundreds of diseases, some very obscure, including the famed Trollian Tonail Fungus, Orc Gastrointestinal Distress Syndrome, and even..." he paused for a moment, and then said, "Zombieism."

Bob fought to keep himself steady. Even Perkder had stopped acting like a 10-year-old girl.

"That's where I've seen you," said Perkder, pointing at the man. "You were at the *CosPlay Posse* convention in Dakmenhem." The guard uncrossed his arms and blanched. "Yeah," said Perkder, nodding. "That's right. You were dressed up as a nurse!"

"Keep your voice down," said the guard, glancing around the room. "Nobody knows about that."

"I do," said Perkder with a smile. "I'm one of the founding members of the *CosPlay Posse*."

"Damn," said the guard.

"You know that we keep records on every person who comes to our conventions. They're private and secure, of course."

"Good."

"I mean," Perkder said, moving his ruby-red shoes this way and that, "you know how sometimes things just happen. You try to keep everything secret, but, somehow, someway, a certain file ends up getting transferred to the dean of a particularly pompous medical school and a poor young lad's career goes up in smoke."

"You wouldn't," the guard said, looking like he was about to sweat.

"Depends on you," said Perkder with a flip of his hand.

"You see, me and my daddy here just want to go back home to Lesang."

The guard's face went sour. "Your daddy?"

"Not *that* kind of daddy," Bob pointed out quickly.

"Oh, right."

A few seconds of silence demonstrated that the guard was weighing his options. It seemed pretty simple to Bob: risk losing his job as a night guard at Yergarn Station or risk losing his doctoral studentship at medical school because of Perkder's threat to let everyone know that the man dressed up as a nurse during *CosPlay Posse* events.

"And you won't tell anybody about the nurse thing?"

"Mister," said Perkder, "not only will I *not* tell, I'll also help you find a much more convincing nurse's outfit for our next convention."

The guard pursed his lips. "Really?"

"I saw a nice pink model just the other day."

He looked around again. "Did it have ruffles?"

"Definitely had ruffles."

Bob wished he'd had proper eyelids so that he could have closed them. He'd also considered removing his ears, which was something he was capable of doing. Instead, he just stood there listening to Perkder and the guard as they went over the intricate details of playing dress-up.

"Excuse me," said another patron, an elderly woman who looked rather perturbed. "Would you mind getting on with it? I'm not getting any younger here, you know?"

"Sorry," said the guard quickly. Then he looked over the papers again, and said rather loudly, "Yes, yes, well, all looks in order here. If you'll just step onto that platform, we'll get you and your lovely daughter to Lesang in the blink of an eye."

"Daughter, my ass," said the old woman. "Put some chains on that Zombie and he'll look like a pimp, and that Dwarf looks like a damn idiot wearing that little girl's outfit. In my day, you'd both be kicked in the shins for dressing so foolishly."

"Right," said the guard before pressing the button to initiate the portal.

PLACES TO GO

*M*odacio was looking back and forth between the width of a particular set of bars on the jail cell and the width of a particular Dark Halfling.

"Not gonna fit," said Grubby tiredly.

"You will if you take your clothes off."

"I bet you'd like that, wouldn't ya?" he said with a sniff.

"Don't flatter yourself," Modacio replied with a laugh. "I'm sure there's nothing on you that I haven't seen on a baby."

"A baby elephant, maybe," Grubby countered. "Anyway, clothes or not, I won't fit through there."

Modacio did another check over the dimensions. It'd be a squeeze, sure, but he could get through with a little effort. Unfortunately, he had the look of someone who wasn't even interested in trying.

She'd have to try another tactic.

"You're probably right," she said with a sigh, flopping down on the bench opposite of him. "I guess we'll just wait here until they take us back to the portal station and ship us to our prison sentences."

"I'm telling you, I'm not going to fit."

"I know, I know," she said, putting her hands up in surrender. "I'm no longer suggesting it. Fact is that we're doomed." She went silent and started drumming her fingers on the bench. "It's a shame, too, seeing that the keys are right there."

"I won't fit."

"Nope," she said, twisting her mouth while nodding sadly. "Like I said, we're doomed."

Grubby sighed. "I'm not a child, you know? I know what you're trying to do. But, like it or not, I won't fit."

"You could at least try," she said in a huff.

"You try first."

She smirked and leaned back against the wall. "Nice effort, little man."

"Hey," Grubby shrugged, "I'm willing to try if you're willing to try."

"You know damn well there's not a chance in hell that I'm going to fit through those bars."

"And I've told you the same about me, but you're not listening so neither am I."

They stared at each other for a few moments before Modacio threw her hands up and said, "Fine, you want to see me naked? Is that it?"

"Yep."

"Sure do," said a man from another cell.

"Me too," said yet another.

"Damn it," came another voice from across the room, "those bastards took my glasses. I can't see a thing. Somebody's gonna have to describe it for me."

"That's it," said Modacio, sitting back down. "I'm not going to put on a full show for everyone."

"Fine with me," Grubby said with a wry smile. "I guess that just means we're *doomed*."

Modacio gave him a dirty look before closing her eyes and taking a deep breath. She knew the little creep could squeeze through the bars. He was merely doing this to get a rise out of her. Fine, if that's how he wanted to play it, she'd play along.

"You win," she said, standing up. "But we do this together. You take off yours at the same time I take off mine."

"Works for me," said Grubby, standing up.

"Awe, shucks," said one the men in another cell, "I don't want to see *that*."

"Me neither," said the other.

"Sure am glad those bastards took my glasses," said the third guy.

They began stripping at the same time. Modacio did her best to make it a non-seductive play. She was completely professional about it. Off came her boots, then her pants, then her shirt.

Grubby followed along, article by article.

"You still have on your underbritches," she announced.

"As do you," he replied with a grin.

"Fine."

Seconds later they were both nude and Modacio learned that Grubby the Dark Halfling had not been kidding about his baby elephant comparison. Worse, it was on the rise.

"Holy heaving mugs of ale," said one of the other prisoners. "Is that thing real? If it is, it'd explain why that midget looks a bit blue. All the damn oxygen must be in that thing of his."

The other prisoner leaned forward. "I thought you said you weren't gonna look—goodness gracious, boy! Are you part horse or something?"

"May The Twelve strike me down," Modacio said with a gasp, blinking a few times and shaking her head. "You were right, Grubby. There's no way you're getting through those bars while carrying that thing."

"Especially after seeing you in the nude," Grubby replied with a wink.

~

"I are Kone," Kone said to a man who was standing at the main gate of a rather large mansion.

"He's with me, Mr. White," said Bledstone.

The man, who was wearing a little white jacket and a pair of green shorts, said, "And he's safe?"

"As far as we know, sir."

Kone frowned, feeling hurt. "I are safe."

"And you're an Ogre, eh?"

"I are, yep."

"Never seen one of you in person, I have to admit. Rather large creatures, I see."

Kone wasn't fond of being called a *creature*, but he let it go. There was no point in starting a fight, after all. Not that it would be much of a fight. The guy was just slightly taller than Grubby and a bit thinner.

"Now," said the man while holding his chin, "I remember once hearing that there were two distinct types of Ogres: mean ones and dumb ones. Which one are you?"

"I not dumb," said Kone, "but I not mean, too. I fink you got wrong infermation."

"Hmmm," said the man. "Well, do you drink fine wine?"

"Not really," Kone answered. "It just taste like funny water that had a foot in it. I like milk, though. You got milk?"

The man nodded. "I'm sure we do."

"Dat's good."

"And you're sure you're not the mean type, right?"

"I don't like hurtin' nobody, mister. Not on purpose anyway."

"Do Ogres lie?"

"Not as far as you know, mister."

"Well, that's true, I suppose."

Kone smiled, feeling smart as the man let him and Bledstone in through the gate and led them toward the sound of music and laughter.

THE UPPERWORLD

*B*ob had no idea what to expect the moment he saw the portal room at Lesang. The room itself was small with little adornment and there was only one guard who was sitting in a wooden chair at a wooden table. He was wearing a blue uniform that appeared to be covered with chainmail. His hair was long and dark, though the top looked somewhat matted. This was likely from having to wear the helmet that sat before him on the table.

Standing up menacingly, the guard slid his hand toward a rather large broadsword that hung by his side.

"Your names?" he said.

"Bob Mermenhermen, and this is my daughter, uh… Perkder Stonepebble."

"Your daughter?" said the guard, doubtfully.

"We're from the Underworld," Perkder offered.

"Oh." The guard looked appeased by that explanation. He smiled genuinely. "Well, then, I suppose that's normal."

"If you say so," said Bob.

"Hmmm?"

"Nothing."

"Do you have papers?" asked the guard.

"No, sir," Perkder jumped in before Bob could speak. "We're actually following a few thieves."

The guard's head shot up. "Thieves?"

"Three of them," said Perkder, looking at Bob for assurance.

Bob said, "A Human, a Dark Halfling, and an Ogre."

"Did they walk into a bar by any chance?" asked the guard with a hopeful smile.

"Uh..." Bob said, taken off guard. "I wouldn't know. We haven't seen them since they left the Underworld."

"Hard to get any good jokes in these parts," the guard replied, deflated. "Anyway, there was some activity up above a little while ago. A few unexpected arrivals came through, or so I'm told. They didn't give me any details."

"We should go and—"

"Now, hold on a second, there," said the guard, again grabbing the handle of his sword. "We're not supposed to let Underworlders up here without papers. I could lose my job for that."

"Wouldn't want that," said Perkder. "I know what it's like to lose a job you love."

"Never said I loved it, really, but—"

"Can we maybe speak to your supervisor?" asked Bob. "That way it's up to him and you'll be off the hook."

"Good thinking for an Underworlder," said the guard, removing his hand from the sword.

Bob was pretty certain he should have been offended by that comment, but he decided to not worry about it, especially after all the atrocities and name-calling that he'd endured by simply being a Zombie.

They walked up a set of stairs that took Bob a while to navigate. Perkder had explained that Bob was elderly and needed a little extra time. The guard said nothing as Bob finally crossed the top step and they went outside.

The air was crisp and the sky was clear. Compared to the Underworld, where there was almost always smog, fog, rain, or cloud cover…at least in Dogda, this place was beautiful, even in the middle of the night.

Bob looked out over the town in the distance and noted many large homes. It was tough to see any details simply through the light of the moon, but from what he *could* see this was a town full of wealthy people. Unless, of course, everyone in the Upperworld lived like this.

Off in the distance Bob could make out a few properties that were lit up. From the top of the hill he could basically just see the glow, but with some of the lights circling this way and that, and a few of those lights changing colors throughout the full spectrum of a rainbow, Bob would guess that they were nightclubs or that there was a party going on.

"Sir," said the guard to another guard, "this guy and his, uh, daughter just came through the portal."

"Another set, eh?" said the older-looking guard. "Underworlders?"

"Yes, sir," said the guard.

"Good job, Rathbone, I'll take it from here."

"Yes, sir," Rathbone said with a quick salute before shuffling back toward the portal room.

"Well," said the older guard, "we're just a landing station tonight for Underworlders, aren't we? I got two of you in the clink and one is down at the party at the end of the road."

"Party?" said Perkder, stepping up.

The guard looked down at him. "You're a Dwarf."

"Yes."

"Lesangians don't much like Dwarfs," said the guard.

"Why not?" said Perkder, looking hurt. "I've never done anything to them."

"Sir," said Bob with as much volume as he could muster, "this particular Dwarf is not like his brethren. He's happy."

"I don't care if he's Dopey, Sleepy, or Sneezy," the guard retaliated, "he's still a Dwarf and we ain't supposed to let them through. And what about you? You look like a pimp."

"I am a...Zombie."

"A Zombie?" The guard backed away and brought his hand to his nose. "Did you say you were a Zombie?"

Bob's shoulders dropped, figuratively speaking. "Yes."

"You're not going to bite me, are you?"

"Not that I'm aware of," Bob answered.

"But he could," stated Perkder dramatically. "That's why I'm with him."

"What?" said Bob and the guard simultaneously.

"I'm here to keep him in check."

The guard kept his face covered. "Keep him in check?"

"Of course," said Perkder, giving Bob a wink. "Everyone knows that as long as there is a Dwarf around, a Zombie can't bite anyone."

The guard squinted. "Is that true?"

"Tell him, Bob," said Perkder.

"Sure," said Bob, thinking maybe the whole hand-in-the-lava thing might not be so bad after all. "It's true. I'll behave as long as my Dwarf is with me."

"That's a new one to me," said the guard. "I'll have to put that in the books. Typically, the people of Lesang want Underworld Dwarfs slapped into jail immediately, but they say that if any Zombies ever come up they should be allowed to roam free. Makes no sense, if you ask me. Seems dangerous, it does. But they make the rules around these parts. I just enforce them. Anyway, we've never had a

Zombie up here before, so if you say that Happy here will help you stay out of trouble, then that will have to do."

"Who's Happy?" asked Perkder.

"I thought you were?" answered the guard.

"Well, I *am* happy, but I'm not *Happy*. My name is Perkder."

The guard shook his head as if trying to clear out some confusion. Finally, he just shrugged and said, "So you're here looking for those other three?"

"Yes, sir," said Perkder.

"The Ogre went down to the party a few hours ago. The other two are in the cells below. Which do you want to see?"

"Ogre," said Bob, recalling how the overgrown ape had taken his hand and placed it in a satchel that he'd been carrying.

"Johnson," the old guard shouted. A young-looking man ran out of the building. The old guard pointed. "These two are looking for the Ogre that came in earlier. Get Master Wizard Redler to adjust them accordingly and then take them down to Mr. White's. You'll find the Ogre there with Bledstone, I'm sure."

"Yes, sir! Thank you, sir!"

"Don't screw it up, Johnson."

"Won't, sir."

"Uh-huh."

PARTY TIME

$\mathcal{I}$t had taken some time for Grubby's "situation" to subside and even then Modacio couldn't help but be in awe at the magnitude of the thing. She hadn't been with a man in years, ever since she went on the run from the Thieves Union, so the visage hanging before her was more than tempting. On top of that, so to speak, she'd never been with any race *other* than Human. Her assumption was that Orcs and Ogres were hung like Grubby and that Dark Halflings, Dwarfs, and Gnomes were hung like crickets. She could only assume that Grubby was an anomaly.

Either way, right now, horny or not, she had a job to do. She had to get the hell out of this cell, find Kone, get to Flaymtahk Island, and get those damn pills made. Then she'd be free and clear of the contract on her head, and then she could pursue a little something more interesting. Or, she thought, giving one more glance in Grubby's direction, maybe a big something more interesting.

With lightning speed, she rushed over to Grubby, picked him up, and pushed him between the bars. He grunted, shocked, but she'd already had his head and shoulders through before he could start to fight. That's as far as she got before he started growing again.

"Can't you control that thing?" she asked.

"Not when a nude woman is pressing herself against me, no. And thank you so much for getting me stuck between the bars like this. It's not humiliating in the least."

"Think about business or something," she suggested. "If that thing goes down you should be able to pull yourself through."

"I doubt it, but I'll try."

Fifteen minutes later, Grubby was through the bars. It would have been sooner, but it turned out that thinking about money for the Dark Halfling was more of a turn-on than having Modacio's nude body pressed against him. It wasn't until she'd mentioned that if one of the guards came down and saw him in such a precarious position, things could go really wrong that he'd lost his happenstance in record time.

Once their clothes were on they went about opening the cells for everyone else, in the hopes that with everyone making a break for it at the same time, they'd get free.

That turned out to be unnecessary, though, since they all just walked casually out of a doorway on the same level.

It led to a waterway just outside the building. A quick climb up a little hill and they were on the main road, heading down toward the end of the street where they could hear music.

"Why are we going down here?" asked Grubby as the other prisoners all went their separate ways.

"If I know Kone," Modacio replied, "he'll be there."

"Why?"

"He loves dancing."

"You're kidding."

"Sadly, I'm not."

~

"That's him, all right," said Bob as they walked into through the gate with a little man who was wearing a white suit.

"He's quite the dancer," said the man as Kone was lighting up the dance floor with a couple of Mr. White's other guests. "He's been shaking his booty all night. Quite the party animal, that one." Mr. White chuckled softly. "Nice enough fellow, too. Friend of yours, you say?"

"Sure," said Bob.

"Well, drinks are on the other side of the pool. There may not be much left since you're getting here a little late. Most of the guests went home about an hour ago." Mr. White then turned toward Perkder. "I do like your shoes, Mr. Stonepebble."

"Yeah? Me too. Very comfy."

The man smiled sweetly and walked away.

"Mr. White is a good citizen," said Guard Johnson as the little man was walking away. "Always helpful."

"Seems decent enough," agreed Bob while keeping his eyes on Kone.

"How do you want to handle this?" Perkder said to Bob.

Bob didn't answer. He merely walked across the dance floor, directly up to Kone, and tapped him on the shoulder.

Kone turned around and his eyes got really wide.

"Hey, yer dat Zombie guy! You look like a pimp."

"Where's my hand?"

"Hmmm?"

"My hand."

"I can't hear you," Kone replied. "Der music is too loud."

"Where's his hand?" yelled Perkder.

"Oh, dat." Kone pointed to a table that sat near the flowerbed in the garden. "It's in my satchel over der."

Bob turned and walked toward the table without saying another word, but Kone sped past him and snatched up the satchel before he could get to it.

"What am you doin'?"

"I want my hand back."

"What?"

"He wants his hand back!"

"You can't just take it," said Kone, looking affronted. "Dat'd be stealing."

Bob opened his mouth a few times, unsure how to respond to that. How was it stealing if it was *his* hand? Besides, they'd stolen it from him in the first place, right?

"It's my hand! I never gave it to you. You just took it."

By now the music had moved to a slow song and Bob's voice carried loudly enough.

"Dat's not true. You was on dat ladder and you dropped your hand on dat street der. I picked it up and put it in my satchel. I even fanked you for it."

"Do you honestly think I would just give up my hand because you asked me for it?"

Kone scratched his ear and then shrugged. "People give me stuff all der time. All yer gotta do is ask, I say."

Bob shook his head and grunted. It made sense, actually. When a 7-foot-tall, musclebound Ogre asks you for something, you tended to oblige. But not if he wants a body part!

"Well, I didn't want to give you my hand. I never wanted to give you my hand. It fell off because I'm a Zombie, and that kind of thing happens all the time."

"Oh," Kone said, looking confused. "I didn't know dat, mister. I fought you was being helpful."

"I wasn't."

"Something we can help with here?" said Bledstone, motioning between himself and Johnson. "If there is thievery involved, after all, we *are* the law."

"This is Underworld business," Bob said, keeping his eyes on Kone.

"Stealing is stealing, regardless of where it is," Bledstone pointed out. "We have a right to do our jobs, you know?"

"Yeah," Johnson jumped in, "we're required to do our jobs and stuff."

"Too bad," came the familiar voice of a woman.

Everyone turned.

Bob saw Perkder standing very still as the blade of a Dark Halfling was pressed against his neck. Beside Perkder stood Modacio and the man in the white suit. His predicament wasn't much better than Perkder's.

"Hi, Modacio," said Kone with a gap-toothed smile. "Hi, Grubby."

"Quit saying our names, you moron!"

"Don't call me a moron, Grubby. Dat not nice."

"Grrr," responded the Dark Halfling.

"You do still have the Zombie's hand, right?" Modacio said to Kone.

He nodded, but said, "Got a problem, though. This guy said he weren't meaning to give it to me."

"A deal's a deal," she stated. "You know that. We talked about it a number of times."

"But him not make a deal, he says."

She sighed. "You have the hand in your bag, right?"

"Yep."

"He dropped it for you, right?"

Kone pursed his lips and looked to be in thought. "Yep, him did."

"A deal's a deal," she said with a shrug.

"Sorry, mister," Kone said, looking at Bob. "She right. A deal's a deal."

"But—"

"Uh-hem," the Dark Halfling said, motioning that Perkder was moments away from losing a fair amount of blood if Bob didn't shut up.

"Right," Bob said, defeated. "A deal is a deal."

"Good," said Modacio with a big smile. "Now that we have an understanding, I believe we'll be on our way." She turned toward the group of people that were all looking on in shock at what was happening. "If you all would be so kind as to sit over there, we'll let ourselves out and nobody will get hurt."

"Sorry, ma'am," said Bledstone, holding up his hand, "but we can't allow any illegal activity in this area. Besides, I believe that both you and your Dark Halfling friend here are supposed to be in jail."

"Yeah," said Johnson, "in jail."

Bob felt concerned at the calmness that Modacio was showing.

"Kone," she said sweetly, "would you please engage your special skill?"

"Which one?" asked Kone.

"The memory one."

"All of dem?"

"We can't risk your technique on the Zombie, knowing how you feel about hurting people, and we know that the Dwarf's head is too hard for you to work with. As for the rest of the people, I think they'll be silent on their own for a good long time, yes?"

Everyone nodded.

"So just the guards, then."

Kone looked around. "Okay, how long?"

"One day should be fine."

"What are you two talking about?" asked Bledstone.

Bonk. Bonk.

Both Bledstone and Johnson fell down in a heap.

"Ooops," said Kone. "I fink I did about a week."

"And our friend in white here?"

"Nope," said Kone. "I not knock his head. He a friend and I promised I not hurt him."

"Fine," said Modacio and then motioned everyone to move to the chairs.

They moved to sit down as the Dark Halfling lifted the key to the main gate from Mr. White's suit.

"Please don't move," Modacio said with a wink. "I would certainly hate for anything bad to happen to any of you."

"You truly are a horrible person," said Bob.

"Probably true, Bob," Modacio said with a shrug. "Sometimes we have to do things in order to save our own skins. Sadly, that may mean we have to do bad things to others. It's nothing personal, I assure you. Well, maybe a little personal. I do enjoy a fine heist, after all. Mostly, though, I'm currently more fond of keeping my head than I am of returning your hand."

Bob grunted at that.

He watched as the three of them exited the gate and then, once the clicking sound of the lock latching into place sounded, he turned toward the man in the white suit.

"I'm assuming you have another key?"

"It's inside," he answered, "but she said not to move."

"Fine, I'll get it myself," Bob said. "Just tell me where it is."

The man seemed conflicted. "Normally the help would be available for things like this, but I sent them home after your Ogre friend arrived...just in case, you know?"

"Not really."

"I don't know how wise it is to move, Mr. White," said a woman who was dressed in sequins. "That woman with the blade seemed rather serious about our staying put."

"Come on, you dolt," said Perkder to Mr. White, stepping between him and the woman who'd just warned him. "The man's hand is at stake, here!"

"But she sounded quite threatening," Mr. White said, leaning to the side and nodding at the rest of the wealthy party-goers.

"Oh, that's it, is it?" said Perkder, removing his wig and showing his normal dark hair. "I'm generally an easygoing Dwarf. I like to make people happy, you know? But sometimes I let the actual Dwarf in me come out. When that happens, somebody usually gets hurt." He turned menacingly toward the man in the white suit. "Now, I'm either going to let the Dwarf in me come out or you're going to tell me where the damn key is. Which is it going to be?"

GETTING TO FLAYMTAHK

I know you're carrying a bit of extra weight in your undercarriage, Grubby," said Modacio, worried that the others would be hot on their tail, "but can't you go any faster?"

"I've got short legs, lady!"

"Kone?"

"No, no, no," said Grubby, but it was too late. Kone had swept him up and they were moving at full speed toward the pier. "Why don't you pick her up, too, you big oaf?"

"'Cause she faster dan me," said Kone, and then added, "and listen, Grubby, I know you got a problem, and I are not making no fun of dat…but please don't poop on me."

"I don't have any damn problem," Grubby replied with a growl.

Modacio could have just gone to the pier that was outside of the house, and that's exactly what she would have done if it weren't for the fear that trying to find a captain who would skipper them across to the island of lava this late at night would prove futile. By moving up the coast a bit, she could try a few different options before the Zombie and the Dwarf caught up with them.

She also didn't want to get too close to the guard station at the top of the hill. Another stint in jail simply wouldn't do.

Looking down one of the ramps, she saw a man sitting on the back of a little boat. She slid to a halt, yelling for Kone to stop and follow her.

The man squinted up at them as they strolled up. Though the lighting in the area was somewhat dim, there was a nice beam that was shinning right on the guy. He looked as though the name "Grubby" would be more suited to him than it was to the Dark Halfling. He had mussy hair, a scruffy beard, and leathery skin. In one hand was a half-empty bottle of booze. In the other hand was a completely empty bottle of booze.

"Whatcher want?" he asked with a slur.

"We need to get to Flaymtahk Island," said Modacio.

The man sat up a bit, though he continued to wobble slightly. "What fer?"

"Personal business," Modacio countered. "But we have money."

"So do I," said the man and then he took a swig from the bottle. "I just don't look li...li...like it."

"Well, I'm sure—"

"You see that how...how...house up on the hill?" He was pointing toward a gigantic white house that had so many levels that it looked like a small hotel in Dakmenhem. "That belongs to me...me...me brother."

Grubby turned his head to look up at Kone. "Can you please let me down now?"

"Oh, sorry," said Kone, putting the Dark Halfling on the ground. "Fanks for not poo—"

"Shut up, already! I don't have a problem!" Grubby

brushed himself off and then looked at the drunk man. "So you're saying that your brother has money."

"What's his is mi…mi…mine," said the drunk, "and what's mine is…hmmm…mine, too, I guess. He don't wa…want nothin' of mine. Says it ain't worth much. But it's mine and so I say that's good enough fer me!"

He took another deep pull from the bottle and squinted at Grubby. "Why are you blue?"

"Is this your boat?" Modacio asked, interrupting the drunk's train of thought.

"Nope," the man said, wiping his mouth with his sleeve. "Me brother's."

"I fought dat mean it yours too," Kone said, looking confused and scratching his buttocks.

The man peered up at the Ogre. "You know what? Yer…yer…huge!"

"Yep, I know dat."

"But yer also right! It *is* my boat…kinda."

"Then will you take us to Flaymtahk?"

"I would be happy to doo…doo—"

"I would prefer you didn't," said Grubby with a grimace.

"Maybe you oughta give him one of your diapers, Grubby," Kone suggested.

Grubby just glared at the Ogre.

"I don't know what yer talkin' 'bout," the man said, frowning. "I thought you wanted me to bring you some…place."

"He simply misunderstood you, sir," said Modacio. "We would love for you to take us to the island."

"Norm…normally, I would be fine with that. But, there's this…thing that you do…don't know."

"What's dat, mister?" asked Kone.

The man burped and said, "I don't know how to guide a boat."

"I do," said Modacio.

"Oh, well, then there ya go!"

He put the empty bottle down, stepped off the boat, took two steps, and then fell flat on his face, smashing the other bottle in the process.

Grubby grunted and said, "Well, may as well take the boat."

Nobody argued, but Kone picked the man up and propped him gently against a wall before they hopped aboard. Kone then snagged the oars from the sides and started rowing them out to sea.

"Too bad we don't have a motor," noted Grubby, peering over the edge of the boat.

"Agreed," said Modacio, settling down in a leather chair near the front. "Hopefully none of the other boats do either."

WHAT HAPPENED?

r. White sat on the bench by the two guards as they finally came around. He had sent all of the other guests home for the night, telling them to remember to keep their word about not saying anything to anyone and explaining that he would come up with a story solid enough to fool the two disabled guards. The last thing he wanted was for those thieves to come back to exact revenge on him due to someone having loose lips.

The knock that the Ogre had given each of them on the head didn't look that hard, but he supposed that any impact from a fist that large would cause some damage.

"What happened?" said Bledstone, squinting through scrunched eyes.

Mr. White thought about this for a moment. Could it have been true that the Ogre was able to erase their memories with a bonk to the head?

"What do you remember?" asked Mr. White with pursed lips.

Bledstone was up on one elbow now, rubbing his head. "Last I remember, I was helping Miss Wedlow pick out some vegetables. She's been a bit ill of late. It was the middle of the day, I think." He didn't look too sure as he glanced at the sky. "Then...I woke up here."

"Hmmm," said Mr. White, nodding.

"Where am I?" said Johnson with a groan. Then he looked up and added, "Mr. White, is that you?"

"It is, my dear boy," said Mr. White. "What's the last thing you recall?"

"Not much, sir. I was going to bed, so it was around noon."

"Bed at noon?"

"Yes, sir. I work the night shift most of the time."

"Ah, yes, right. Go on."

"Well, I was about to put my head on the pillow and then I woke up here." Johnson shook his head lightly. "I remember having a headache when I was going to bed, though."

"This is all very interesting, indeed," said Mr. White, thinking it might be best to keep his cards close to his vest.

To have an Ogre around with such power could prove quite useful to his normal, well, adventures. He wasn't sure if all Ogres had this particular skill or not, but he made a mental note to look into the possibility at some point.

"What happened to you both is just as much a mystery to me as it is to you, officers."

Mr. White then recalled all of the stories he'd heard regarding alien abductions and the like over the last couple of years. Eying these two, he felt assured that they'd be gullible enough to believe anything he told them.

"I saw a bright light in the sky," he said, carefully. "A disk-shaped object, somewhat metallic in nature. It was absolutely silent. I wouldn't have even known it was there were it not for the interesting array of lights it had bandying about its hull. They caught my eye as I was sitting outside having a cup of tea." The two men's eyes were wide with fright. "Suddenly a brilliant beam of white light shone down on this area of my courtyard. It stayed alight for about ten seconds and then disappeared. The craft moved off over toward the sea, slowly at first, and then it zipped away before I had time to even blink. I walked over to this spot and found you two lying here unconscious."

Johnson audibly gulped. Bledstone just gazed out toward the sky over the sea.

"You don't think they did those...*things* to us like the stories all say, do you?" asked Johnson worriedly.

"Things?"

"You know," he said, gulping again, "liking sticking things in us."

"Ah, that I couldn't say, young man. You appear to be sitting comfortably, though."

"Hmmm? Oh, no, not *that*, Mr. White. I meant needles and the like."

"Oh, yes, of course, you mean *those* stories. Well, I suppose you'd need to see a physician to clarify that, wouldn't you?"

"I guess so," Johnson replied, his eyes dropping to the ground.

"A flying saucer?" Bledstone said in disbelief. Then he smiled. "A real flying saucer picked us up? We'll be the talk of the town, Johnson."

"We will?"

"Think about it. We'll be celebrities. Everyone will want to hang out with us. Isn't that right, Mr. White?"

"As you say," Mr. White said, thinking how he would have to bribe the guards at the main tower to accept the story as stated so that nobody would be the wiser. "You'll be the talk of the town."

THE BOAT

*B*ob and Perkder had looked everywhere for the three thieves, but they were nowhere to be found. There were so many boats in the area that they could have been hiding anywhere. But that made little sense to Bob. Why would they be hiding? It made more sense that they'd be getting to the island.

"They're already gone," Bob said finally, as Perkder came back into view, returning from his search of the smaller boats.

"We need a boat," said Perkder in agreement.

All the boats were dark, except one, and its light was pretty dim. Taking a chance, Bob and Perkder walked over and knocked on the side of the boat.

"Hello?" called Perkder. "Anybody home?"

A set of eyes appeared in the window where the light was. It was a man of middle years, if Bob was any judge. He opened the door.

"What can I do ya for?" said the man, looking them both over carefully.

"We're looking for passage to the island."

"Flaymtahk?" said the man.

"Yes," replied Bob.

The man yawned and stretched. "Why would a sharp dressed man and his daughter want to go to Flaymtahk Island?"

Bob and Perkder looked at each other for a moment. Then they both nodded and whispered, "Wizard."

"Hmmm?"

"Nothing, sir," said Bob, "it's just that my, uh, daughter here is doing an experiment for school and it requires an element from the island. Since everyone knows it's safer to go to the island at night—"

"It is?"

"Most assuredly," said Bob as if he were an expert on the subject. "Going during the day is lunacy."

"Never heard of that," said the man while stretching. "Either way, I suppose I can take you two over there, if you really have need, but it ain't free."

"How much?" said Perkder.

The man nearly jumped. "Your daughter's got a pretty deep voice there, mister."

"How much?" repeated Perkder.

"Two silver should do it."

Bob dug into his pocket and pulled out a few coins, but then realized that they were Underworld coins. He showed them to Perkder who waved at him to put them away. Bob did. Perkder pulled out a couple of his own and handed them over.

"Excellent," said the man, who was now all smiles. "My name is Yeb C. Lubb, but my friends call me Yeb, or Lubb, or Y.C.L., or Y-Clubb, or Clubb, or—"

"Yeb will do," Bob interrupted. "I'm Bob and this is Perkder."

"Nice to meet fine people," the man said with a wink. "Now we just need a means of propulsion."

"What?"

"My rowers don't start work for another couple of hours."

"Then why'd you agree to take us at night?"

"I didn't. I just said that I could take you two over there. You were the ones talking about the whole night thing."

"It was rather implied that we need to go at night, though."

Yeb shrugged and gave an innocent look.

"Libby dee, Yebby C!" a voice called out.

Bob turned and saw the wizard that had been up at the guard station.

"Hey, Red," said Yeb. "Good to see ya!" Then he turned back to Bob and said, "Forgot about that one. You can call me Yebby C, too."

"Nook dook a bang bing," the wizard was saying, wagging a finger at Bob and Perkder.

"You're fugitives?" Yeb said, looking shocked.

"You can understand him?" asked Bob, looking more shocked.

"We go way back."

"Ah. Well, no, we're not fugitives."

"Nook dook a bang bing," Red said again, crossing his arms.

"No, we're not," Bob replied, assuming he was still calling them fugitives. "The Human, the Dark Halfling, and the Ogre are the fugitives."

"What are you talking about?" said Yeb with a squint. "There ain't no such thing as Ogres and Dark Halflings."

"Iwablip dah stone stone," Red said before turning to give Bob a sharp look.

"Right, sorry…uh…that's just what we call them because one is short and one is tall and they're both thieves."

"Gotcha," said Yeb.

"And we're chasing them now, which is why we need your boat."

"You and your daughter are chasing fugitives?"

Bob gummed his lip for a moment and then said, "Yes."

"What about the school project?"

"That was a ruse."

"Ah," said the man. "And what's a ruse?"

"We were trying to trick you."

"That's not nice."

"Sorry. Look, we need to get over there. It's literally a matter of life and death. Can you help us or not?"

"Gebble ding sleppy doo?" the wizard said to Bob.

Bob whispered, "I honestly don't know what you're saying, sir, but the truth is that those thieves have my hand and if they drop it in the wrong pit of lava, I'll die."

"Ahhh…nord gude."

Yeb was looking them over again during the conversation. He was grunting and mumbling something to himself.

Master Wizard Redler gave Bob one more glance and then stepped up to Yeb while jingling his purse. "Derby roo ard onda curptuh ordee nook dook a bang bing."

"Reward, eh?" Yeb said. "How much we talking?"

"Hmmm…ord…mebbe dwo glayd."

Yeb's eyes opened wide enough that they nearly added light to the area. "One or two gold?"

"Mebbe."

"I'll do it!"

"What about the rowers?" Perkder asked.

"Yeah," said Yeb, snapping his fingers. "That's a problem."

"Hmmm." Red pushed them all out of the way and looked over the boat. He knelt down and rapped a few times against the hull. Then he stood up and said "Hmmm" a few more times before finally snapping his fingers. "Ooh hoo! Pred coob dah sip sip a zoom zoom."

"A motor? On my boat?" The captain of the vessel scratched at the back of his neck. "Sounds dangerous."

"Mebbe."

"I don't know," Yeb said, looking unsure.

Everyone stood silently for a moment.

"No nook dook a bang bing, no glayd," Red pointed out.

"Yeah, I know," said Yeb. "I could really use that glayd... erm...gold, too." He sighed heavily and put his hands up in the air. "Fine, fine. You can put a motor on the boat. Just promise me you won't sink us, yeah?"

"Mebbe."

FLAYMTAHK

*G*rubby had just finished sending his latest report to Teggins when the heat of the island began to hit the boat. He hadn't really put much thought into how they were going to handle the temperatures. It was an island of lava and volcanoes, after all.

Modacio was still standing at the front of the boat and she didn't seem all that worried about the rising heat.

Kone had been singing from the moment he put the oars in the water. Grubby assumed that it had something to do with keeping his cadence. Surprisingly, the oaf had a pretty decent voice, and his diction wasn't marred even slightly as he sang the words. It reminded him of how some cultures had massive accents while talking, but seemingly none when singing.

Go!
We find ourselves in the row.
Go!
Our pirating, ho ho ho!

Go!
The water dips and dives.
Go!
The waves! They give me the hives!

There were apparently enough verses to keep a crew singing for hours because Kone hadn't repeated himself once since they'd left port. Of course, most of the verses made little to no sense, but few rowing songs did. Where he'd learned the song was beyond Grubby, and frankly the Dark Halfling didn't really care. But even he had to admit that having the constant chant had helped the time pass. Once or twice he'd even caught himself mumbling "Go!" along with the Ogre.

"Okay, Kone," Modacio shouted, "cut the singing. We're almost there."

"Aye, aye, Cap'n!"

Modacio cracked her neck from side to side, gave Grubby a funny look, and then announced, "Three more pulls ought to hit us onto the beach. Hold on."

The boat came to a halt, jolting its passengers in the process.

Grubby righted himself while smelling the stench of something in the air. Sulfur, maybe? Methane? He looked at Kone suspiciously. That smell hadn't been there before.

"Wasn't me," said Kone, as if knowing what Grubby was thinking.

"It was me," said Modacio, rubbing her stomach. "The sea gives me the wind something fierce."

Kone and Grubby shared an "ew" moment.

"Let's go," Modacio commanded, jumping over the edge of the boat and into the knee-deep water.

Kone picked up Grubby without even asking, jumped in,

and then set him on dry land. Whether Grubby wanted to be irritated at being picked up or not, he couldn't argue that being on dry land was more suitable than being wet. Then again, at least being wet would have helped cool him off.

"According to my studies, we just have to get past this first set of stones and the heat will dissipate. Something to do with how The Twelve created the place."

They followed her past the stone and, sure enough, it began to get a little cooler. After another hundred feet or so, it was actually quite pleasant.

"Here we are," Modacio said, motioning toward three lava pits. "One of these is our ticket to riches."

"Which one?"

Modacio didn't answer. She just started unpacking her supplies, setting each element down and carefully twisting off their respective tops. She then unfolded a piece of paper and pointed at it and each of the items in front of her.

"Everything is in order," she said, standing back up.

"So which one is the right pit?"

"You already asked me that."

"And you didn't answer me."

"Correct."

CATCHING UP

They'd gotten across to the island very quickly, due to the magical motor that Master Wizard Redler had installed. When they'd pulled up to shore, Yeb hand-cranked a ramp into position and they all began to file out.

"I'll stay here," announced Yeb. "No point in me going near that lava."

Bob turned around and said, "I'd rather you joined us. I wouldn't want to be stranded here, after all."

"Are you questioning my ethics, sir?"

"Plet snip snap chebbeh."

"Well, sure, *you* can question my ethics, Red, but I know you. I don't know this guy."

"Don't think of it as me questioning your honor, Yeb," said Bob smoothly. "Think of it as me not knowing *you* very well as yet." Then Bob looked at Red and said, "Besides, it would be nice to have someone to help translate."

"And there'll be two more silver in it for you, if you do," added Perkder.

"Oh, well, why didn't you say so?"

They moved past the rocks with Red in the lead. Bob

couldn't explain why, especially since he was from the Underworld—where magic was a thing of abnormality—but he was glad that the little wizard had joined them. He made Bob feel safe, or at least protected.

At the bottom of the ravine stood the three thieves.

Kone was holding Bob's dismembered hand as Modacio snapped off a finger, making Bob wince, even from this distance. She then dropped the finger into an iron pot and started pouring the contents of other containers on top of it.

"We have to stop them," said Perkder, picking up his pace as they moved down the hill.

Bob was the last one to arrive, being that he'd simply fall to pieces (literally) if he lost his footing. Fortunately, the splint that Perkder had built for his leg was still holding up. He'd need it on for probably another week at least before he could resume walking normally.

"Stop!" commanded Perkder.

Modacio ignored him, continuing instead to work on whatever it was she was doing with Bob's finger.

Grubby pulled out a blade and took two steps toward Perkder, who, in turn, froze in place.

"Oh, hi again, you guys!" Kone said happily. "We was just getting ready to do dat boner stuff wif your hand, weren't we, Grubby?"

"For the love of The Twelve," said Grubby, pinching his nose at the top, "do you ever shut up?"

Kone frowned. "You not nice, Grubby."

"No, I'm not."

Red stepped up and pointed. "Nook dook a bang bing."

"Right, we know," Bob said as he finally reached the bottom of the hill. "That's why we've been following them. They stole my hand."

"A deal is a deal," said Kone. "Ain't dat right, Modacio?"

She grunted in reply, keeping her eyes on the paper in front of her.

"There was no deal," Bob said frantically. "I never wanted you to have my hand. It fell off me because I was trying to get away from you!"

"But at dat party you said der was a deal."

"That's only because your Dark Halfling friend here had a knife up against my friend's neck."

Kone frowned. "Dat true, Grubby?"

"He's lying," said Grubby. "You know how Zombie's lie."

"Oh, right," Bob said, sarcastically. "We lie all the time."

"Dat true, too, Grubby?"

"Unless he's lying again," said Grubby. "Never can tell with Zombies."

"Hmmm."

"Kone," said Perkder, stepping up. "You seem relatively smart."

"Seriously?" said Grubby.

"Yep, mister. I are."

"You also seem to be pretty nice."

"My ma raised me right, dat's why."

"Your ma, eh?" said Perkder with a wink toward Bob. "I can't imagine your ma would ever want you to do anything to purposefully hurt anyone, would she?"

"Nope. She'd tan my hide, she would."

"If they put that hand in the wrong lava, Kone, do you know what will happen to Bob?"

"What?"

"He'll die," said Perkder seriously.

"Don't listen to him," Grubby said tersely. "He's lying too."

Kone looked at Grubby and then back at Perkder and then back at Grubby. "Yer sayin' dat Dwarfs lie, too?"

113

"All the time. That's why they get along so well with Zombies."

"Uwar bunka melroons," Red stated, folding his arms.

"He just called you all a bunch of morons," said Yeb, seemingly pleased to have something to contribute.

"I know what him said," said Kone. "And I are not no moron."

"Nep doo," Red said, waving dismissively at Kone. "Dem."

"He said that you're not a moron, but the rest of them are."

"Who you calling a moron?" Grubby said, taking a step toward the wizard.

That's when Bob saw it. Perkder was about to make his move. One instant he was standing just out of reach, but the next he'd launched himself full force, head first into Grubby's side. The blade was knocked free from the Dark Halfling's grip, landing a few feet away in a splash of lava, where it was instantly consumed.

Bob took two steps toward Modacio, but she swiftly pulled out a blade of her own and pointed it directly at Bob, not once taking her eyes from the paper she was reading. He backed away.

"Somefing don't feel right about all dis, Modacio," said Kone. "Dey seem awfully angry about stuff. Ain't deals supposed to be good on all sides?"

"Not always, Kone," she said irritably. "Just keep them in check while I finish, will you please? I only have to put in the secret ingredient, the final step, and I'll be ready to put this in the pit."

"What if dis guy is right? What if you put it in da wrong pit? What happens?"

"He'll die," she said, obviously too consumed by what she was reading.

"He'll die?"

"Um-hmm," she replied, and then stopped and peered up with an "uh oh" look on her face.

"You not tell me dat before, Modacio," Kone said seriously. "You know I don't go in fer killin' nobody. Dat wasn't in our plan."

"What I meant wasn't that he'd really die, Kone," she said, backtracking. "I mean that his hand will die. Yeah, that's what I meant."

"I fink you're lying, Modacio," Kone replied, looking unhappy. "I fink bof you and Grubby are da ones really lying to me. I fink dat da Zombie and da Dwarf is tellin' da truth."

"A deal is a deal?" she replied hopefully as Kone's monster of a fist came down and bonked her on top of the head, causing her to fall straight down while dropping the contents of her container.

As Kone walked over and picked up Grubby, bonking him on the head, too, Bob watched as the container that held a piece of his hand began to roll toward the lava pit.

He moved far too swiftly for a Zombie to safely move, but he had little choice. If that container went into the pit, he'd be dead in an instant.

"Bob, no!" yelled Perkder, but it was too late.

Bob had pushed himself up onto a rock and was ready to leap toward the container.

That's when the splint cracked and fell off, causing his leg to snap again.

He fell sideways into a large pit of lava on the other side.

A moment later he was completely submersed in a pool of fire.

WHOLE AGAIN

s he lay in lava, Bob fully expected that everything would come to an end. He would burn up in a flash, and that would be that.

But he didn't feel any burning sensation at all. There was a bit of a tingle, and then he felt something really odd: strength. He hadn't felt much in the way of strength for years.

He gripped his good hand. It was strong. It felt normal!

Pushing himself to a seated position, he saw the faces of everyone. Perkder, Red, Yeb, and Kone were all gazing at him in horror.

"Why aren't you dead?" said Yeb.

"You look different, Bob," said Perkder. "Like you're not really fully a Zombie anymore."

"Blay beck dwan, qark!"

"What?"

"He said to lay back down, quickly," said Yeb, shocked.

"Doo et!"

Bob didn't need that translated. He merely took a deep

breath and lay himself back in the lava. Again, it didn't hurt. Not even slightly. If anything, it felt amazing.

He felt a splash and then something moved to attach to the end of his arm. It was his other hand. Obviously it had not made it into the pit as Bob had assumed. Life soon pulsed in it as well, causing him to fill with joy.

The Zombieism was being healed!

It was a miracle.

He would be able to help all of the Zombies throughout Ononokin to get their normal lives back. *He* would have his normal life back. No more taunts. No more fear. No more buying cases of deodorant and scented candles!

Finally, after what seemed like hours, he heard an audible "Ding."

He sat up again, and then, with a strength he'd not recalled since his youth, he jumped up and stepped out of the pool. Everyone backed away, looking at him in utter shock.

"What the hell is going on?" asked Yeb.

"Hmmm," said Red. "Himma gorta freget allbootdis."

"Why do I have to forget?"

Kone walked over and bonked Yeb on the head. "Der. Him won't remember nuffin' dat happened tonight."

"Hmmm," said Red, looking up at Kone. "Useful."

"Yerp."

"Bob," Perkder said, his eyes flashing with joy, "you're healed. I mean, completely healed. You're no longer a Zombie!"

Bob was beside himself with happiness. He felt wonderful. He reached up and touched his face and his hair. It was all back. There was even a full set of teeth in his mouth as he ran his tongue over them. He could blink!

"I don't believe it," he said, smiling genuinely for the first time in years. "This is amazing."

They laughed and danced around, hopping and laughing. Even Red and Kone joined in on the merriment.

It was then that Bob noted that Modacio and Grubby were stirring from Kone's bonking.

He stopped dancing. "What about them?"

"Hmmm," Red said, his smile fading. "Nook dook a bang bing."

And that's when Kone told the story of how they all got up here and why Modacio was doing what it was she was doing.

A NEW LIFE

The boat was quickly zooming back toward Lesang as Perkder took the helm and steered it along. Bob was standing up next to him, feeling the mist of the ocean spattering across his face.

Red was talking with Yeb, feeding him a bunch of information about what had happened. Kone seemed to be okay with the little lies being fed to the sea captain, which Bob assumed meant that Kone understood the need for secrecy regarding the Underworld.

At the back of the boat, Modacio was sitting with Grubby. They were gazing into each other's eyes like a couple of love birds. It was a bit unnerving, truth be told.

"I thought you couldn't make anyone fall in love with magic?" Bob said to Red as Yeb went into the cabin.

"Whedee gert det?"

"Him said, 'Where'd ya get dat?'," said Kone, who appeared quite adept at understanding Red's odd language.

"I don't know," answered Bob. "All the fairy tales from the Underworld say that about magic. Of course, we're also told that magic is evil and scary and all that."

"Wep...derts messly trood."

"Him said—"

"I got that one," Bob answered with a smile as he moved down close to Kone and Red, lowering his voice. "But what about the contract on Modacio's head?"

Red grunted and said, "Beh! Demno gorna bredda um fiilmoot wez dip."

Bob blinked a few times and looked at Kone questioningly.

"Not sure, but I fink dat he's saying dat nobody is going to bother wif dem up here. Not worth da risk."

"Yerp."

"Ah, but won't they know he's a Dark Halfling?"

Kone held up a finger to stop Red before he started. "I got dis one," he said. "Red made dem fink der bof Human. Dey also don't know dat dey was thieves. Red's gonna set dem up to live in Lesang in peace. Nobody gonna know what der deal is, especially dem."

"But he's blue."

"Oxergeen oodleboop."

"Him have a breaving problem," said Kone, smiling. "Him not get enough oxergen. Make him blue looking."

"Kind of seems like they're getting a good deal for being criminals," Bob said, feeling somewhat unnerved. "They could have killed me."

"Din vrooory! Dell ber clenin der shat as ere leevin."

"What?"

"Him said not to worry 'cause dey bof fink dat der jobs is to clean up crap for living."

"What?"

Yeb had returned and he was rubbing his temples.

"Dem gonna clean up crap," Kone repeated.

"I heard you," Bob replied, "I just don't understand what that's got to do with them paying for breaking the law."

"Criminals in Lesang work in the sewers," Yeb explained. "It's their penance. Wizards like Red here cast a spell on them so that they actually love the job. They don't know it's a bad thing, really, but everyone else does. Kind of sick, if you ask me, but then again, I float around on a boat all day, so what do I know?"

Bob smiled.

"What about Kone?" Perkder asked.

"Red asked me to work wif him on stuff. Promised it'd be honest stuff, too, not stuff like Modacio did."

"That's great, Kone," Bob said, and he genuinely felt that way. Through all of what had happened, Bob never felt that the Ogre had a bad bone in his body. He was merely tricked into believing that what he was doing was all part of a deal.

"What about you?" asked Kone after Yeb walked up to the wheel.

"Me?" said Bob, pursing his lips. "I think I've just found a way to make a living helping Zombies get their lives back. I have the unique perspective of knowing what they're going through, and I know how to get them healed. Feels like I have little choice but to follow my new life's calling."

"Gerd moon….gerd moon."

"What?"

"Him says yer a good man."

"I don't know about that," Bob said, thinking back over his years, "but I do know that I'm a fortunate one."

EPILOGUE

 odacio and Grubby shared the title of Employee of the Month more times than anyone ever had in the sewage system on Lesang. They'd even started a medium-sized family as the years went by.

As a favor to Kone, Master Wizard Redler had gone to the Underworld to have a word with Teggins regarding the two former thieves. With the help of Kone, the wizard explained that if anything were to happen to either the Human or the Dark Halfling, he would personally put out a Wizard Bounty on Teggins's head.

Teggins begrudgingly agreed, but only after Kone's particular skills were utilized to bonk the memories out of a few particular members of the law that had a lot of dirt on the Thieves Guild.

Bob and Perkder had spent the next 10 years working through the bureaucracy of getting the Underworld and Upperworld to a state of allowing Zombies to come up through Lesang and across to Flaymtahk Island in order to seek healing. With the help of the wealthy residents of Lesang, they nearly eradicated Zombieism from all the members of the Underworld. There were a few that had no interest in being healed, which was beyond odd, but some people just seemed to relish self-loathing.

Perkder took his portion of the proceeds to take the *CosPlay Posse* to the next level, bringing it into the Upperworld and expanding it into many more regions in the Underworld. With a bit of backing and business acumen that he'd gotten from a few Lesang merchants, specifically Mr. White and his two new assistants, Bledstone and Johnson, Perkder was now collecting annual dues, running events, and making a killing on the market. He had gotten so wealthy, in fact, that he now had his own mansion in Lesang.

Bob's life had become one of legend.

He was revered by many as being the Zombie savior. He had even written the book, *Bob the Zombie*, in an effort to show others what the life of a Zombie was really like. It hit #1 on the charts and stayed there for nearly a year.

The only thing that Bob was missing was immortality, or at least something close to it.

"Are you sure you want to do this?" asked Perkder as Bob lay on the table in Viq.

"It was a one in a million chance the first time, Perkder," he replied with a smile. "To happen twice would defy the odds completely."

"Yeah, but if it *does* happen again, Red says that the lava treatment might not work."

"We don't know that for certain."

"He seems pretty smart about these things."

Bob grimaced. "You have a lot of years ahead of you,

Perkder. I've got maybe thirty. This will give me a shot at another thousand years."

"It's your life, Bob," Perkder said finally, patting his friend on the shoulder.

~

It happened again.

Fortunately, Red was wrong. The lava treatment *did* work effectively.

Bob tried once again each year through illegal channels since Vampires weren't allowed to infect people with their disease except every 100 years, but he just kept contracting Zombieism every time until he finally gave up at the ripe old age of 83.

"It's been an interesting life," he said to his old friend Perkder. "I hold the Milgness Book of Underworld Records for turning into and being healed from Zombieism more times than anyone else. That's something, at least."

"Doubt that record will ever be broken," Perkder said with a smile.

"Hope not."

"You also gave Zombies everywhere a way to be healed; don't forget that."

"Yes, true."

A shadow covered the doorway and a hulking figure came inside.

"Kone?"

"Yerp. It me. Sorry yer about ter die and all. Dat's sad."

"Especially from my point of view," admitted Bob.

Red stepped inside a moment later, pointed at Perkder and Kone, and said, "Gert oot."

"What?"

"Him said we gotta get out."

"Oh."

As they left, Red shut the door behind them. Then he darted around the room and shut the shades on all the windows and, for some reason, glanced up the chimney.

He cleared his throat and pulled out a small vial.

"Dreenk."

"What is it?" asked Bob suspiciously.

It seemed to take a lot of effort, but Red slowly said, "Whut...dooo...yer...care? Yer...gorna...die...anyhoo."

"True," said Bob, thinking how he'd spent years being bitten by Vampires, to no avail.

He threw back the contents of the vial and felt heat radiate through his bones. The pain was incredible, but he felt life seeping back into his body.

"What's happening!"

"Yer gooten yinger!"

"What?!?!?"

~

Apparently, through the funding of everyone in both the old Zombie community and the residents of Lesang, Bob was given the gift of youth. His body had returned back to age of 23.

They all felt he had deserved a longer shot at life because of all the good he'd done for the people of Ononokin.

Bob took the opportunity to travel and see the world. He had decided that, instead of wasting his life constantly chasing immortality, he was going to focus his efforts on *living* a life of adventure, seeking thrills every chance he could.

Unfortunately, he died a year later after being stepped on

by a forty-foot Gorgan during a sight-seeing tour in the Gorgan Mountains.

～

One year after his death, Perkder, Red, Kone, and numerous people from Lesang had taken Bob's ashes and spread them over the lava pits on Flaymtahk Island.

～

Rumor has it that, early in the morning on the island of lava, the voice of Bob Mermenhermen—the former Zombie who regained his Humanity, the man who had helped hundreds of Zombies be cured of their ailments, and the man who touched so many lives in such positive ways, some of whom didn't even deserve it—can be heard yelling the final words he'd said on the day of his demise:

"Don't you dare step on me, you overgrown...urng...."

A LETTER FROM DR. BUNK MOZATTO

*H*ey Reader,
     Just a quick note to say thanks for picking up this book. Bottom line is my Zombie business went through the roof after Bob got all them Zombies cured and that only happened because you guys bought this book and helped make me famous.

It turned out that a lot of Zombies suffered from PZSD (Post Zombie Stress Disorder). The once-Zombies got it in their heads that people were still treatin' them like Zombies. Some of them even went as far as to pay people to call them names and throw stuff at them! Weird, right?

Anyway, 'cause of this and 'cause I was shown in the book as being *the* go-to-guy for all things relating to Zombieism, I'm making a bundle at my clinic. At this rate, I'll be able to pay back all of my student loans and retire within the next 20 years!

But, listen, I also do other types of psychiatry, so if you're ever in the area and in need of a shrink, look me up. Bring a copy of your book with you and I'll even sign it…for a small fee, of course.

Right. Well. Thanks.

-Dr. B. M.

Thanks for Reading

If you enjoyed this book, would you please leave a review at the site you purchased it from? It doesn't have to be a book report... just a line or two would be fantastic and it would really help us out!

John P. Logsdon
www.JohnPLogsdon.com

John was raised in the MD/VA/DC area. Growing up, John had a steady interest in writing stories, playing music, and tinkering with computers. He spent over 20 years working in the video games industry where he acted as designer and producer on many online games. He's written science fiction, fantasy, humor, and even books on game development. While he enjoys writing lighthearted adventures and wacky comedies most, he can't seem to turn down writing darker fiction. John lives with his wife, son, and Chihuahua.

Christopher P. Young

Chris grew up in the Maryland suburbs. He spent the majority of his childhood reading and writing science fiction and learning the craft of storytelling. He worked as a designer and producer in the video games industry for a number of years as well as working in technology and admin services. He enjoys writing both serious and comedic science fiction and fantasy. Chris lives with his wife and an ever-growing population of critters.

Crimson Myth Press offers more books by this author as well as books from a few other hand-picked authors. From science fiction & fantasy to adventure & mystery, we bring the best stories for adults and kids alike.

Check out our complete book catalog:

www.CrimsonMyth.com

25174550R00083

Printed in Great Britain
by Amazon